CLAIMED BY THE BERSERKERS

THE BERSERKER SAGA
BOOK 5

LEE SAVINO

SILVERWOOD PRESS, LLC

FREE BOOK

Get two secret Berserker books, Bred by the Berserkers and
A Berserker Birth, available exclusively to you:

CLAIMED BY THE BERSERKERS

"You're ours now, lass. We're claiming ye."

My mind and body are weakened by the curse of my magic. My three sisters have mated with Berserker warriors, but I am too frail to be a bride.

One night, three warriors break into my home. They steal me away.

Now we're on the run from the pack. These warriors tell me I belong to them, and that they'll never let me go. To convince me, they spend hours giving me endless pleasure...

But there's an evil power preying on me. It wants me for its own, and none can stand in its way.

Except the Berserkers.

Note: *Claimed by the Berserkers* is a MFM ménage romance starring three huge, dominant warriors who make it all about the woman. There are NO M/M scenes. Read the whole best-selling Berserker saga to see what readers are raving about...

1

The Grey Man stood on the edge of the field, watching me. I'd seen his kind before—waiting and watching with the unblinking stillness of a snake. I called them 'Grey Men' because their skin was just that, grey and leathery. They were all tall and rail-thin, hunched forward with sunken eyes fixed on me.

I hadn't seen one in almost a year, but it didn't surprise me that one was stalking me now, when I was out at the market. In the past, they showed themselves when I was alone, without protection.

I wasn't alone anymore.

Swallowing hard, I ducked between the rows of market stalls, putting distance between myself and the Grey Man. He might follow me, but he'd keep to the edge of the market. As long as I didn't stray from the populated field, he wouldn't come close.

My twin sister's head bobbed ahead of me as she bent to examine one villager's wares. As I headed for her, people averted their eyes or hurried out of my path, not for me, but for the massive warriors tailing me. My bodyguards: the huge warriors known as Berserkers.

"Look, Fleur," my sister called. She also had a Berserker guard, a hulking giant who was also her mate. He hovered over her shoulder, casting a shadow, but she mostly ignored him, and I did the same to my two guards; tall and heavily-muscled men named Arne and Erik.

As my sister and I and the three Berserkers gathered at the table full of bright bits of cloth, the owner of the stall gulped and paled. Behind him, his wife shrank behind her loom, hiding herself and her children from us and making the sign of the cross.

Muriel didn't seem to notice.

"This ribbon would be perfect for your hair." She held up the shining spool in rich teal. Dutifully, I bent my head and let her study the color against my braid. I bit back the comment that nothing would help my dull, blonde hair—limp and thin after my last season of sickness.

"It's lovely," Muriel prattled on, and I agreed with less enthusiasm. I didn't need new ribbons or finery—I lived in a mountain cave surrounded by a pack of brutish warriors, not a king's court—but I pitied the vendor and his frightened family. A purchase would reward them for their trouble, even if it could not allay their fears.

Muriel's mate loomed over her, his scarred face, shaved head, giant axe and glowering expression at odds with her sunny smile. Muriel was so happy to be out at market. A year had passed since we'd both been taken by the Berserkers, and this was the first time we'd been allowed a trip away from the warrior's remote home. Even though she'd found her place in the pack with her new mates, Muriel had missed civilization.

"Such vivid color," Muriel praised the stallman, who

gripped the edge of his table as if it was the only thing keeping him from falling to his knees. "How do you do it?"

"'Tis a secret recipe, made with spices from the east, and herbs from this very island."

"Fascinating," Muriel said. "And so beautiful, Fleur, with your light hair." Even though Muriel and I were twins, she had dark hair like our eldest sister Brenna, while mine was mostly hay-colored like our sister Sabine. "We'll take this for you, and the purple for me." She pointed, but when the vendor moved close enough to hand her the spool, Muriel's mate let out a growl.

The vendor dropped his offering onto the table with a clunk. "Forgive me, my lord," he said in a shaking tone.

"It's all right," Muriel took up the spool and measured out how much she wanted herself. "My husband is protective."

Flinching at the clink of the warrior's weapons, the owner of the stall named his price.

We left the vendor a cowed, but richer man, and walked to another stall roasting large hanks of meat. Muriel skipped along, her fingers threaded with her mate's huge ones. She chattered as if he weren't glaring at every man who unwisely gazed too long at her soft beauty.

I stayed quiet, watching the Grey Man out of the corner of my eye. He'd moved around the field so he could keep me in his sights, but hadn't come any closer. With the warriors surrounding me, I was safe, but my stomach twisted with a sense of foreboding. The Grey Men hadn't dogged my steps since the Berserkers took me and Muriel. Before then, when my sisters and I lived alone in a hut on the edge of a small village, I'd see their ghostly forms all the time. I hid from them best I could, but their mere presence seemed to leave me sick and drained.

"Muriel," I whispered when our three guards were distracted. "Do you see that man?"

"Where?" She kept her voice down.

"There, on the edge of the field. He's looking at us."

Muriel glanced back. "Beyond the butcher's stall?"

"Yes, at the edge of the animal pen." The cattle had all drifted to the far corner, away from the Grey Man. None of the villagers went near him, either. I described the strange watcher and Muriel frowned. "I see an old man leaning on the fence, and the cows in the pen, but no one with grey skin, like you described."

The Grey Man was leaning on the fence. He straightened when he saw me glance back at him.

"Look away," I hissed.

"Fleur, who is it?"

"I don't know."

I closed my eyes as Muriel set a hand to my forehead.

"No fever," she said. "Are you sure you saw such a creature?"

"Yes. Never mind." Drawing my sister's attention to him would only put her in danger. Better for me to face my horrible vision alone.

I picked at the food our guards brought, unable to eat. Muriel went back to chatting with her mate, giving me worried looks from time to time. When I was young, I'd asked my mother and adults around me about the disturbing things I saw, and quickly learned that they weren't real. Now I only asked Muriel, and swore her to secrecy. My two other sisters worried enough about my health.

As I sat, trying to ignore the Grey Man, my head pounding as if the sunlight was trying to break through my skull. My stomach rumbled but not with hunger.

"Something wrong, lass? Do ye not like the meat?" one of my guards leaned over me.

"'Tis fine, sir," I kept my eyes down. Rough, tattooed hands reached for my bowl, and my skin prickled as it always did around this Berserker. He was the first warrior I'd met when he burst into our hut and carried me off into the night--Erik, a Norseman who'd lived long enough on the island to pick up a light brogue. He had neatly trimmed black beard and tattoos running up his muscled arms.

"Something smells rotten. What do you think, Arne?" Erik passed my bowl to my second guard, a bronze-skinned warrior with a bald head and a hooked nose like the beak of an eagle. Arne was neither a Norseman or of Alba, but from far off lands I'd never heard of. With his dark coloring and exotic beauty, he stood out from the other pale-skinned warriors. A feather hung from his pierced ear.

"I smell it too. It's not the meat." Arne raised his head, scanning the market. My stomach clenched in panic. Instinct told me the Grey Man was dangerous, but I couldn't allow the Berserkers to scent him--their violent rage would overtake them. If they faced an enemy here, in a crowded place, innocent people might die.

"Perhaps we should visit the other side of the market," I blurted, and started walking. My back prickled; the Grey Man was still watching.

The wind shifted and the rotting smell mingled in the scent of roasting meat followed me, but faded when my two Berserker guards crowded closer.

"Is there anything else you wish to shop for?" Erik asked, falling into step next to me. I took two strides for his one.

"No, sir." There was nothing I needed. My sisters all had mates—a pair of husbands each—to look pretty for. With my waifish form, and sickly complexion, I couldn't look pretty anyway.

"Nothing at all? We have enough gold to buy ye anything ye need." He swept out a hand to include the whole bustling market.

I sighed. I was supposed to choose cloth for a new gown. My sisters were making it for me. Midsummer approached. My last fever had ended a moon ago, and soon I would be expected to take a Berserker to mate. The Alphas were deciding who would claim me. Last time, they'd hosted a huge Games for my sister Muriel and she was given away. Fortunately, she seemed content with her two mates.

For some reason, Berserkers claimed their mates in pairs, and my sisters and I were the only women who could break the curse on these warriors. We had a gentle, latent magic that tamed the monstrous beast that gave the Berserkers their strength and took from them any chance of living in peace. The pack had been on the brink of going mad before they found us, but now they had hope of living a normal life.

Muriel, Sabine and Brenna had all been claimed. Soon it would be my turn.

If I lived long enough.

The Grey Man stalked around the edge of the field again, tracking me.

Picking up my pace, I rounded a corner and ran into a large black dog, a magnificent beast that came well up to my waist.

Not a dog. A wolf. Berserker.

The people around us quieted and moved quickly away. I didn't know what made them more nervous: the great, brutish warriors frowning and handling their wares, or the massive wolf strolling between the stalls.

"Gunnr," I smiled. This was the only Berserker I ever felt comfortable talking to. He was always in wolf form.

The warrior wolf butted against my legs gently, and I buried my hand in his thick fur. He didn't move out of my way, so I knelt to look in his face and met his golden eyes, unlike any ordinary wolf. Unnatural and intelligent.

He stared at me as if he knew something was wrong.

"Fleur? Where were you going in such a hurry?" A shadow fell over me as Erik and Arne flanked me once more.

"Nowhere. I just thought I saw—" a pain pierced my head and I squinted against the sun. Something dripped down my face; I touched my nose and my finger came away red. Blood.

Gunnr whined.

I raised my head. The Grey Man stood not five feet away. He had flat, dull eyes. Dead man's eyes. He raised a bony hand and pointed at me.

My skull throbbed again.

"Fleur, what is wrong?" My guards spoke over one another. "What is happening?" Metal rasped as they drew weapons.

"No, it's nothing, don't hurt anyone—" My stomach lurched as I mumbled the words. The world tilted, my feet no longer on firm ground. My legs buckled as the shakes took me.

I grabbed at Erik, opening my mouth at his wild expression, trying to tell him I was fine, I'd had these seizures before. My head flew back, my teeth knocking with each convulsion.

"Fleur!"

"Quick, grab her—"

Strong hands held my arms. A firm body was at my back, gentle arms caging me.

The shakes subsided. I was in Arne's lap, head cradled in the crook of his elbow.

"What happened?" Muriel rushed up.

"She's all right," Erik said, smoothing my hair back.

"I've got her," Arne echoed, and lifted me. "We're leaving. This excursion is over."

2

As the group moved towards the forest, I rested my forehead against Arne's muscled shoulder. His skin smelled rich and earthy, with a touch of spice. I raised my head and met glittering eyes. His Berserker rage was close to the surface, threatening to break free. Still, he was beautiful, his golden eyes gilt in the shadows of the deep woods.

"Something frightened you back there," he said softly. "You were fine when we first arrived."

"It was the heat," I whispered, dropping my gaze. "The sun and all the people."

His eyes glittered. "Don't lie to me. You were afraid. I could smell it. You saw something at the market that spooked you."

Before I could deny it, he called to Erik.

"Take her." Arne handed me off to the tattooed warrior, and headed back towards the market.

"What's he doing?"

"Just going back to find out what's spooked ye." Erik

cradled me closer. "Dinnae be worried about him, lass. He can take care of himself."

I gnawed my lip as Erik's determined strides took us further into the forest. "You don't have to carry me. I can walk."

"I know, wee Fleur." But he didn't put me down.

I threaded my arm around his shoulders. This time I was careful not to look the warrior carrying me in the eye. Wolves had strict rules that dictated what place each one held in the pack. Looking a stronger wolf in the eye was considered a challenge for dominance, and would end in a fight, or a punishment in front of the whole pack. Even though my sisters and I were female and cherished, the Alphas warned us that until the Berserkers were more stable, their savage nature—what they called "the beast"—tamed, the rules still applied. The only wolves my sisters could gaze at were their mates.

After a few minutes journeying on the path between the trees, he stiffened, and left the worn trail. Behind us, Muriel and her mate had disappeared.

"Where are we going?"

"Arne saw something he didn't like in the market. We're changing course."

"But—" my protest died away. The Alphas had warned my sisters and I of the dangers of being alone with one of the warriors, but I was helpless to cross this warrior. Better not to challenge him.

"Your sister will be fine with her mate. We're splitting up."

Erik left the path and plunged between the thick pines, ducking under the branches while I hung on.

"Do not worry," he said, as calm as if we were on a pleasant trip and not weaving through the trees as if something was chasing us. "Whatever it is, Arne will make sure to divert it. He is the best scout in the pack. We're often sent on missions together."

Instead of meeting his gaze, I stared at his lips, full and perfectly formed. "You're his warrior brother?"

"Aye. He saved my life, I saved his. The bond formed between us then, and we are closer than brothers."

I swallowed. My sisters had explained some of the bonds — the psychic lines that tied members of the pack together. Over time, pack magic allowed two warriors to form closer, stronger bonds between each other. These 'brother bonds' helped keep them alive. If one warrior started to succumb to the Berserker rage, his warrior brother would be there to balance him and pull him back from the brink.

Unless the beast consumed them both, and they went mad until they died.

"Calm yourself, lass. There's nothing to fear in these woods, except, perhaps me." The smile he gave me came with a very white, very pointy pair of teeth.

It made my heart beat faster, but not entirely from fear.

A shadow stirred the underbrush.

I clutched at the Norseman. "Something is following us."

"'Tis only Gunnr."

Even as Erik spoke, the wolf darted out of the thicket and back in again, making no sound on his giant paws.

"He runs behind to guard us. You're safe, wee Fleur."

I said nothing. A year ago, I feared the Berserkers more than any of my visions. Today, I wasn't so sure. My sisters told me that though they now loved their mates, at first they'd been frightened by them. Of course, from what I could tell, when Berserkers claimed their mates, the women weren't given a choice.

Now my sisters were all mated, it was my turn.

When we reached a sun dappled fern grove, Erik's steps slowed.

"We can stop here to rest."

A tall figure stepped out from behind a tree, and I startled back. He stepped into the light, a feather caught behind his ear in addition to the one hanging from his earring.

"Arne," I breathed in relief. Smiling, he came to crouch down near me. His teeth were white against his bronze skin.

"Miss me, little flower?"

Reaching up, I pulled the feather from behind his ear. I'd never seen such a mesmerizing pattern.

"Keep it," he said.

"Where are the others?" Erik asked.

"Halfway to their home near the mountain. It was as I suspected. Whatever the evil presence was, it didn't follow them. It wanted Fleur."

Gunnr growled and Erik's voice turned thick and guttural. "What was it?"

"I don't know," Arne said. "Ask her."

"Did you see it?" I asked.

"No. It cloaked itself somehow from me. But I felt it linger on the edge of the path where we took you. Then it moved through the market like an evil wind. Humans avoided its path."

"Muriel saw it. She thought it looked like an old man," I said.

"What does it look like to you?"

I described the Grey Man, and waited for the warriors to scoff. Instead, they exchanged grim looks.

"Whatever it is, it has power," Arne said. "I felt its malevolence."

"We rest here until we are sure it is not following. Then we return home to the pack," Erik announced.

"I'll set up a few wards," Arne said. Gunnr loped along with him as the bald warrior walked the perimeter.

I curled my arms around my legs, still feeling a little sick. Whatever the Grey Man was, Arne was right, it had wanted me. I would be in its clutches if the Berserkers hadn't been guarding me. The other times I'd spotted the Grey Men, they'd lingered, watching me and my sisters, but never approached. If I had known it was going to attack, I would've run. If it was after me, I put everyone in danger.

My head still throbbed. I wiped at my nose with my sleeve, hoping there was no dried blood.

Erik knelt in front of me. "Let me." He took my chin and tipped up my head to wash my face with a wet cloth. His motions were gentle for such a burly warrior.

"Thank you," I said when he was done, hoping he'd back away. Something about having him close made my cheeks heat.

Tattoos twined over the lean, corded muscle of his bare arms. His leather jerkin stretched across the muscles of his chest. He was a Berserker, a powerful warrior centuries old. Fast, brutal and monstrously strong, yet as rugged and handsome as a human man. Since the day he'd broken into our home and carried me off, he'd been fascinated with me.

His eyes narrowed as he studied me and I studied him.

"That thing—the Grey Man—made ye sick."

"I'm often sick. It's nothing new."

He studied me. "Ye try to hide your illness."

"My sisters already know I am weak. They have their own mates now. I do not wish to worry them." I pressed my lips together. They didn't need to know the truth, that I had seen my own death. I would not live much longer. I was grateful that I'd lasted long enough to see all my sisters mated and happy.

"Ye do not take care of yourself," Erik said, and pressed a bit of dried meat into my hand. "Ye need to eat." Catching my wrist, he directed it and the strip of meat to my mouth. When I didn't take a bite, he tsked at me.

My brows knotted together even as my pulse tripped under his firm grip. "Are you supposed to touch me?"

"Ye like it." He grinned.

I refused to be baited. "The Alphas warned my sisters and me against showing favor to any one Berserker. It will make the others jealous, and cause problems. If the pack finds we've been spending time together alone, they will be upset with you."

"Worried about me, lass?"

"I don't want to cause fights." I took a bite of the meat and he let go of me, but still hovered close.

"Your mere presence is enough to cause a fight. Every unmated warrior wants to be with ye. But dinnae worry, lass, my warrior brothers can hold our own in skirmishes with the rest of the pack." He nudged my arm, a silent order for me to keep eating.

"As for us touching ye now, we're only seeing you home safe, warm and fed. No fault to be found. 'Tis only us three, and we are warrior brothers. We share a bond and there is no room for jealousy. If you belonged to one of us, you belonged to all of us."

I swallowed my mouthful and frowned. "I don't belong to any of you."

At this he only smiled and tucked a strand of hair behind my ear. Heat lingered where his fingers brushed my cheek and temple.

He held another strip of meat to my lips. "Eat, wee flower."

My stomach flipped at his closeness and firm tone, but I managed to get a few bites down.

"Here," Arne squatted beside me and presented me with my favorite food. "Honey cakes."

"You like these." Erik said.

I nibbled on the edge of one. "You've been watching me."

"You've noticed us watching you," Arne smirked and ran a hand over his bald head. With his exotic coloring and eyes, he really was beautiful.

Too late I remembered to drop my gaze.

"It's all right, lass." Erik sounded amused. "Ye can look at us."

"I thought it would arouse the beast. I did not want to tempt you."

"Too late," Arne murmured.

Erik leaned closer. "The beast enjoys your attention."

I propped the honey cake at my mouth so my hand would hide my flushed cheeks.

"Look at me, Fleur," Erik purred, and sent shivers up and down my spine. "I dare ye."

Biting my lip, I did. Gazing into the golden depths, I lost myself.

"Good lass," the bearded warrior encouraged.

When Arne's hand brushed my shoulders, I startled and froze like a frightened rabbit.

"Easy," he soothed.

"I still don't think you should touch me," I muttered. I wasn't afraid of them, not quite. Heat curled through me as if he'd set a brushfire that started on my skin and rushed through my body, warming the core of me. My nipples tingled.

"Why not? Do you like it when we touch you?"

They could scent whether I told them the truth.

"I don't know." I crumbled the honey cake with my fingers. "It is forbidden. The pack hasn't chosen a mate for me."

Erik lay his hand over mine.

"Haven't ye heard? The Alphas met last full moon and decided. Ye have until midsummer's night to meet everyone in the pack. And then you are to choose a mate."

My last bite stuck in my throat, making me sputter. "What?"

"Did they not tell ye?" Erik glanced at Arne, who shrugged.

"Perhaps they are waiting until the day is closer, in case you become sick. At midsummer, you will be wed. The entire pack waits upon your choice."

I lay my hand on my stomach, already feeling ill.

"I DON'T UNDERSTAND," I asked Muriel when we were back safe at the mountain. The pack had given me a whole chamber when they brought me to their home. The rooms had been carved into the side of the mountain by creatures long gone. My eldest sister Brenna had her own chamber with her mates and children. Muriel lived nearby with her own mates, and visited often. "I thought the Alphas would give me as a prize to a strong warrior, just as you were."

"Be happy, Fleur. The Alphas are allowing you to choose a mate." Was there a touch of bitterness in Muriel's tone?

"And if I do not wish to choose one?"

Muriel pursed her lips. "Then the Alphas will choose for you."

I rubbed my head, which hadn't stopped throbbing since

the incident with the Grey Man. "Forcing us to wed Berserkers...it is madness."

"It is necessary."

"I am not fit to be a mate." I hadn't had a seizure since the market, but the entire pack knew of my sudden illness, and the unknown danger that had tried to follow me. We were banned from visiting the village until the pack knew more about the threat.

Yet another reason for Muriel to resent me.

"I am the weakest of the sisters."

"It doesn't matter. You will choose a mate. they need you to. Something about us, our powers, it allows their beast to sleep. We balance their violent rage."

I huffed. "Why don't they just give me to the whole pack to share, a different Berserker each night?"

Muriel's eyebrows shot up. "If you asked for that, they would grant it."

I sighed. My twin was always so serious. "It was a jest. I don't want a mate, much less a whole pack of them."

"Well, you will have to choose." Muriel folded her hands in front of her primly, the picture of duty. She was the strong twin.

I'd never been strong. Illness, visions, and now enemies: I was weary of it. Perhaps it would be good for me to die young.

It seemed I would not escape this life without having to at least choose a mate.

Since the Alpha's announcement, the warriors who guarded me--and they were always different men--didn't leave me alone. They gave me flowers, gold arm rings, and the softest animal pelts. At meals, they piled honey cakes in front of me until I was sick of the things.

All the attention made me wish I could slip away to die

alone, like an animal. Or just disappear forever. My sisters would mourn but they would never know my true fate.

If I was brave, I'd tell the pack the vision of my death. My body, stiff and still in a tomb. Though I hadn't seen the Grey Men, I knew they were part of my demise.

THE DAYS LENGTHENED and I waited to see more Grey Men. Visions of them filled my dreams at night until I barely dared to sleep. My eldest sister Brenna commented on how pale and sickly I looked, and convinced her Alphas to move me to a freshly built lodge at the foot of the mountain. They reasoned that there I could enjoy the fresh air, and be courted by the pack more easily.

At first I feared the Grey Men even more, but as the moon waxed and waned, none appeared. Whatever magic the Berserkers had, it kept the sinister beings away. A reason to be grateful for my new life as part of the pack.

But my headaches continued, as did the nosebleeds. I found food less and less appealing. I did not sleep at night, so I dozed in the day, and woke shivering from nightmares.

I hid my sickness as best as I could, but before long Brenna and her Alphas called for Sabine, who lived some leagues away. My blonde sister arrived with her two mates, the Alpha pair from the Lowland pack. She fussed over me where I lay in the lodge, weak from fasting.

"A fever, but nothing like I've seen. How long has she been listless?"

"She's been ill before," a male voice murmured. One of the Alphas.

"Never like this," Sabine corrected. "Whatever this fever

is, it's not responding to the usual herbs I give her. She's thinner, too. Are you not feeding her?"

"Of course they're feeding her," Sabine's mate chastened her.

The Highland Alpha continued, "Her decline started when the pack began courting her in earnest. Perhaps the pressure of having to choose ..."

"We waited as long as we could before we told her she must take a mate. We can wait no longer. The pack needs her," another Alpha said.

"No one will be able to mate with her if she dies," Sabine snapped. My second eldest sister had a short temper. "Leave me to do my work."

The voices blurred together before fading away. Sabine made me sit up and drink some broth. She and Brenna bathed me and packed poultices on my heated skin. The lodge filled with the scent of burning healing herbs.

But my fever did not break. I did not know how many days passed with them caring for me, sitting vigil and waiting for the sickness to take its toll.

"I'm dying," I wanted to tell them. "Prepare a pyre." The Grey Men did not need to come close to me to cause my death. Whatever spell the last one had cast at the market, it lingered. The sickness burned deep in my bones, chapping my lips, turning my skin dry as old leaves.

My sisters fretted over me, and spoke in hushed tones. They wanted to call the witch, but were afraid of letting her close to me in my weakened state. The Alphas weren't sure whether the witch was friend or foe.

My sisters slept in shifts, only leaving my side when their mates pulled them away to eat and renew their strength. When I asked them to leave me alone, Muriel cried, but all three honored my request.

That night, I woke to a shadowy person leaning over my bed, and jerked back feebly.

"Be still," a deep voice caressed my ears. Dark hands raised a candle and illuminated the black brows, gold eyes, and striking face of the familiar Berserker.

"Little flower," he said in a grave voice, and lay a hand on my forehead. He smelled of cedar and spice, and another fresh, cold scent, like a winter's night lit only by starlight.

"Arne," I mouthed his name, but did not have the energy to say more.

Outside a wolf howled, its sad voice joined by two or three others.

"I don't have much time. Your sisters are resting under the care of their mates, but I still had to sneak past your guards." He knelt next to the bed, reaching into the small leather bag he wore around his neck. "My great grand-mother was a wise woman. She had magic of the earth. She taught me how to ward off evil." Smoothing back my hair, he touched a twist of wood and dried leaves to my forehead and lips before laying the talisman on my chest. "I believe you took on an evil spirit at the village market."

"It's happened before," I whispered. "The Grey Men come. They try to take me. I fight as much as I can—"

I coughed, and he laid his large hand over my chest, pressing on the talisman. The rattle in my lungs ceased, but he kept his hand there as my body relaxed under its warm, protective weight.

"You will not have to fight any more. My brothers and I watch over you now."

"You do?"

The candle's flickering light caught the edges of his smile. "We do. You are under our protection."

With a weak hand, I touched his where it lay over my heart. "Why?"

"Because you belong to us." He squeezed my hand and turned it over, placing the ward in my hand and closing my fingers around it. "Enough. Rest now." His lips brushed my cheek. "No more sickness or suffering. You will rest." My body relaxed at his command. I fell into sleep so quickly, I thought I dreamed the tall warrior turned into an eagle that flew away through the smoke hole in the roof of the lodge.

AT DAWN, Sabine crept back to my side. I'd hid Arne's gift under my hip. She was so happy that the fever had broken, she did not question why. By noon I was eating and drinking normally, and in the next few days I regained much of my strength.

The moon rose and shone light into the hole at the apex of the roof, but the eagle did not return. Nor did Arne. I fingered his talisman under the robe that covered me. My sisters insisted on staying the nights with me, but I slept better when I was alone. I imagined Arne lying next to me, a strong arm holding me against his body.

I had no more dreams of the Grey Men. Instead, I dreamed of Arne and Erik, with the wolf Gunnr at their side.

TWO NIGHTS BEFORE MIDSUMMER, the Alphas came with Sabine at their side. The pack still expected me to choose a mate.

"She's too weak," Sabine argued.

"No, I can do it," I said, but my voice was so soft, they spoke over me.

"You must delay—she needs to recover. She needs more time."

"We do not have more time," one of the Alphas exploded from his seat and paced the lodge, tearing a hand through his hair. "The pack grows desperate, needy. They are fighting—every day there are more fights."

"I can do it," I put as much power into my voice as I could. It rang in the rafters and everyone looked at me. "You need me to take a mate. I will do my best. I will choose one of the pack...soon."

"Fleur, are you certain?" Sabine leaned forward. One of her mates, a fierce warrior with blue tattoos, put his hand on her arm to hold her back. "You don't know many of the pack."

"I will do my best."

"Your courage does not go unnoticed, Fleur," one Alpha said. "These warriors hold out all hope that they will find the woman who will tame their beast. As far as we know, you and your sisters are the only four women on the island with that ability."

"I understand."

"We have assembled many of the warriors. From the Highland pack and Lowland Pack. Good men. You will choose one to claim as mate," the Alpha explained.

"Or two. Remember the warrior you choose may have a warrior brother. Their close bond will allow them to share you," Sabine's tattooed mate added.

"I can choose any warrior in the pack?" I asked.

The Alphas hesitated before answering, "Any warrior who is strong enough to take you as a mate. We eliminated those who are struggling and may soon be overtaken by their beast."

"Tomorrow we will bring you to the field to watch the games. Not for what you are thinking," the Alpha held up a hand. "You will not be given to the winner."

A moon or two ago, the Berserkers had all competed for my sister Muriel. The strongest of them had won her hand in battle.

"We wished to give you a chance to watch the warriors. Perhaps walk among them and greet them."

"Can you do this, Fleur? Are you strong enough?"

Inwardly I sighed. I was strong enough to walk the field and speak to the warriors, and told the Alphas as much. But I could not choose a mate. It would give him too much heartache when his bride didn't live through another season.

The next day Sabine and Muriel came to prepare me. They braided my hair into a crown, and frowning and fussed over my slender body. Finally they dressed me in a soft underdress and a gown of cream.

"Fleur, you look lovely." My twin couldn't keep the surprise out of her voice.

"A little more food, and rest, and you'll be a beauty to outshine us all," Sabine said.

"Thank you," I said, though the reflection in the bathing water contradicted her. I was too thin, with dark circles under my eyes, but I was alive, and my mind was no longer haunted by the Grey Man's curse.

"Please," I held up the feather I'd plucked from Arne. "Will you weave this into my hair?"

"Of course." My sisters seemed happy I'd made a request, though Sabine studied the feather carefully first.

I took a moment of privacy and slipped Arne's gift into a

pouch of my dress before presenting myself to my sisters. "I am ready."

"Fleur." Muriel squeezed my hand. "You may choose whoever you like. Is there a warrior who catches your fancy?"

"No." Hard to imagine any Berserker catching my 'fancy.' They weren't boys from our village competing for a chance to hold my hand at a dance. They are deadly warriors seeking a mate they would claim for life. Muriel had always been a romantic, even more so now that she had a mate.

"Maybe one that you enjoy speaking to?" Sabine pushed.

I sighed. They would not give up until I gave them a proper answer.

"There is one. Arne. With the feather earring."

"The Moor?" Sabine perked up.

"The warrior who first captured you?" Muriel pressed her lips together.

"Yes." Arne and Erik had taken turns carrying me.

"You care for him?" my twin had struggled during our kidnapping, and been knocked unconscious. Though she didn't admit it, she despised most of the Lowland Pack for the way our captors first treated us. She'd never believe that I was friendly with the men who'd carried us off.

"I do not care for him. I merely know his name."

"I will ask after him." Sabine rose. "At least you will recognize one face at the Games."

But when we reached the field there was no sign of Arne, Erik, or even Gunnr.

"Where is Arne?" Sabine blurted before I could ask her not to. Her mates, the two Alphas of the Lowland pack, exchanged a look.

"Why do you ask for him?" her tattooed mate growled. Face stony, he clamped a hand around her upper arm. I stilled in fear, but Sabine rolled her eyes and swatted at him as he pulled her closer.

"Calm yourself, wolf. I asked on Fleur's behalf. You need not be jealous."

The warrior relaxed. "Arne is with his warrior brothers. They are scouting for the evil that attacked Fleur at the market."

The Alpha's attention swiveled to me. "Do you have interest in Arne and his brothers?"

"Brothers? I thought the brother bond only formed between two wolves," Sabine frowned.

"In most cases it does, but Arne, Erik and Gunnr share a bond, all three. They are the only Berserkers to do so, and it has saved Gunnr's life."

"Gunnr?" Sabine sucked in a breath. "The wolf who attacked me?"

"Yes," her Alpha mate said, and drew her into his arms. "Fleur, when we assembled your potential suitors, we banned any who might be unstable. Gunnr succumbed to the Berserker rage and tried to attack Sabine. Without Arne and Erik helping him, he would've been sentenced to death."

Another Alpha spoke up. "Unstable wolves were banned from seeking your hand in marriage. They will not make suitable mates."

"Aren't those the wolves who need me the most?"

"No, Fleur. We can't risk one of them losing control of his beast."

'Losing control of his beast.' A poetic way to say the warrior would go mad, succumb to the Berserker rage, and kill everyone and everything in its path, friend or foe. A powerful madness that made winners on the battlefield, but disaster everywhere else.

"We only allowed wolves that are strong enough to resist the Berserker rage," the Alpha explained.

I nodded shallowly. I had no reason to feel disappointed. There was no reason for me to choose Arne, Erik and Gunnr, though I knew them better than any other Berserker. Just because I was more comfortable with them didn't mean it would be easier to explain the truth that I was hiding from everyone: that I had seen my death. It didn't matter which Berserker I chose, it would not change my fate. Their long awaited mate would be dead within the year.

"There are many warriors here to choose from, Fleur," Sabine said with false brightness. "You will certainly find another Berserker you prefer above the rest."

On the field, men and wolves alike clashed in a mock skirmish. Even Berserkers play was violent and bloody.

I spent the next two days on the dais overlooking the field, fingering Arne's talisman in my pocket and fending off my sister's questions about which wolf I liked best. During breaks in the Games, the Alphas escorted me through the throngs of battle-hardened men with gold eyes. I couldn't bring myself to look closely at any of the warriors. They'd lived over a century, waiting for one such as me. How would I choose?

A GOLDEN MOON rose on midsummer eve.

"Hunter's moon," Sabine's Alpha said as we walked back to my lodge after a long day on the field watching the Berserker Games.

"Honey Moon," Sabine corrected. "Fleur, will you be all right alone tonight?"

"Of course." Judging from the sly, excited glances

between Sabine and her Alphas, they couldn't wait to adjourn to their private quarters.

"You will not be alone," the Alpha corrected. "We have posted a guard, of course."

He and my sister left holding hands. I barred the door. If there hadn't been two giant Berserkers in front with torches, I would've been tempted to sneak away. Tomorrow I must choose a mate.

I washed my face by the light of the moon. The girl in the water looked sad and wild with the feather in her hair.

"I cannot choose," I said to her. "I need more time."

I'd just lain down when an angry roar rang out, just outside the lodge. Fear tingled down my spine. The sound came from outside, and was cut off quickly, followed by violent snarls and sounds of fighting.

I scrambled to my feet as the lodge doors splintered, flying inwards.

"Who's there?" A half scream, torn from my throat.

Darkness met me. Someone had knocked out the guards and snuffed the torches out in the ground.

I shrieked as a thick blanket came over my head. I thrashed and ripped at it with my hands, but couldn't dislodge it. My attacker lifted me. Fear filled limbs heavy and almost out of my control, I pushed at the giant form, and he clutched me closer. The cool night air on my bare foot shocked me, and I went wild, jerking in my captor's arms as if a fit had taken me. The cloth he'd wrapped me in trapped most of my movements, but panic gripped me and I fought all the harder.

"Be still, wee flower." Erik's voice was muffled through the cloth, but his command gripped me all the same. I stopped fighting.

"Erik? What are you doing?"

From the wind on my skin, he was running at an amazing speed, jumping and twisting while holding me close and being careful not to jar me.

"Hush now. I got ye." His speed slowed to a stop, and he pulled the blanket away. We were in a deep part of the forest, close to a river. The sound of rushing water blended with the crickets and occasional hooting owl. "We're stealing ye away from the pack, Fleur. Gunnr made a distraction. Arne is scouting for us." Moonlight glinted off his canines as he smiled.

"Why?" He set me down and I backed away a little. My teeth chattered as they did when I was deeply afraid. Was this what the Alphas meant by 'unstable wolves'?

"We're helping ye make your choice." He paced the perimeter of the clearing.

"You can't do this," I sputtered. "The Alphas—the pack—"

"They'll be upset." Erik seemed calm, though his eyes shone golden in the darkness. "They'll try to track us. But Arne has a little magic; his great-grandmother was a witch. He is able to disrupt the pack bond and give us some cover, for a little while." He knelt and struck flint to a pile of wood. The clearing showed signs of a ready made camp, with a few bedrolls, a water skin and weapons. The three unstable warriors had planned this.

As Erik built up the bonfire, I backed away further, but stayed in the circle of trees. It would do no good to run. I could only wait and hope these Berserkers were not insane. If I provoked them, their beast might consume them completely—and I was the closest victim.

The fire was a healthy blaze when a soft wind hit my face. Above my head, great wings blotted out the silvery moon. A bird landed close to the fire, an eagle that transformed into a man with piercing eyes.

"Arne?" I gasped.

"Welcome, little flower." He strode to me, his powerful body naked but for a loin cloth. I froze as he bent to kiss my cheek. His lips were hot on my skin. Straightening, he grinned at me and I gaped at him. "No kind words for your rescuers?"

"She thinks we kidnapped her," Erik said.

"You're not our captive unless you truly don't want to be here," Arne said. "And you've always enjoyed our company, haven't you, Fleur?"

"She smells of fear." Erik cocked his head, eyes flaring brighter. "The scent is delicious."

"I shouldn't be here," I protested in a small voice. "The Alphas will not like it."

"The Alphas are the least of our concern. They will see reason. The rest of the pack..." Arne shrugged. "They will feel as if we've snatched a prize from them. I give it a day before the weaker ones lose control and break from the pack to hunt us down. Better if we do not stay here too long."

"Not too long. Just enough for Fleur to get some rest." Erik crossed to a pack hidden at the base of a tree, and drew out a cloak made of many furs sewn together. "Here," he approached me. "Take off your dress, and wrap in this."

"What is that, brother?" Arne asked.

"Tonight we'll set a false trail using her clothes. They'll follow what they believe is her scent. There are herbs in this pelt to mask her sweetness." Erik turned to me. "Go on, lass, and change."

Numb, I set down the robe Erik had given me. Besides kidnapping me, these wolves did not seem crazed, just determined. But would the sight of my flesh trigger their beast?

My hands shook as they went to unfasten my overdress.

Arne nudged Erik. "Turn around."

"What?"

"Turn around and let her strip."

Looking unhappy, Erik did so. Arne nodded at me before he followed suit.

I took my clothes off quickly, before they changed their minds about giving me privacy. I kept on my shift and shrugged on the cloak.

"I'm finished," I told their broad backs.

Erik picked up my clothes from the ground. "I'll buy ye another dress, lass. Once we are safe, you can have as many as ye like."

Arne came forward. With gentle hands he drew the edges of the cloak together and fastened the stays. "One day you will enjoy being naked in our presence, even desire it. Until that day, I promise you are safe with us."

His murmur made me shiver, despite the warm summer night and the heavy fur cloak. Up close, his half naked form seemed more powerful, the line of his muscles perfectly etched in his arms, legs and massive trunk.

"Fleur?"

I couldn't find my voice, so I nodded.

The bushes crackled nearby as Gunnr pushed through them and joined us, tail wagging. Unable to face the intent stares of the other two Berserkers, I dropped to my knees and hugged the midnight wolf, trembling a little.

He licked my face, and I found more courage and turned to the two warriors.

"What are you doing? Why did you take me?"

"The Alphas told ye to choose a mate by midsummer,

did they not?" Finished with the fire, Erik dusted his hands and came towards me.

"They did." If I hadn't been tucked against the large wolf, I would've backed away from the predator in Erik's eyes.

"But you did not know who to choose," Arne rumbled.

"I...I cannot choose yet. I need more time."

Erik and Arne's big bodies loomed over me. My heart pattered faster. Gunnr nuzzled me until I wrapped an arm around his neck.

"Dinnae worry, lass. You no longer need to make a decision." Erik spread his hands. "If you willnae choose a mate, your mates will choose you."

"I don't understand."

"You're ours, now, Fleur," Arne said in his deep, soft voice. "We're claiming you."

"Cl-Claiming me," I stammered. "Why?"

"Because you're ours." With a hand on my arm, Erik drew me up between him and Arne. The two pressed closer, caging me with their hard bodies. Tingles went through me.

"Soon, you will understand."

"Understand what?"

Arne brushed a lock of hair from my face. "That we are made for one another."

I ducked my head and he caught my chin, his thumb brushing my lips. Lightning sizzled through me.

"Please," I whispered.

"Please what, Fleur?" Erik bent his head. Crowded between the huge warriors, I laid my hands on either man's chest to put some distance between myself and their powerful bodies.

Mistake. Heat poured through me just from that slight touch. I snatched my hands back as if I'd been burned, and backed away.

They let me go, but swiveled to follow. Heads weaving and eyes glowing, they looked more predator than man. If they choose to hunt me, I'd have no chance.

Spreading my hands, I appealed to reason. "You can't do this. When the pack finds out, they'll kill you."

Erik cocked his head to the side, a small smile playing on his lips. "Then we better not let them find us."

From what I knew, nothing could stop a Berserker—except another Berserker. As frightened as I was by these three, I did not want to see them torn apart by the pack.

"So we're to run forever?"

"No." Arne said. He also seemed amused. "Just until you decide to choose us."

"I cannot choose a mate."

Erik moved, and Arne mirrored him, stalking me until the back of my legs hit Gunnr. I was pinned between the three.

Erik winked. "It'll be our pleasure to convince ye otherwise."

3

After a few hours, we were on the move again. I'd slept a little resting on Gunnr in his wolf form. Even now I dozed, my arm wound around Erik's neck. The wind on my face told me how fast the Berserker was traveling.

At dawn, we crested a bare hill and there was nothing but forest and fields for miles and miles. The sun climbed in the sky and still Erik carried me as if I weighed nothing. Every so often, the great eagle flew over us and the black wolf slipped out of the underbrush.

We came to a great river and Erik followed it until it broke into two smaller tributaries. He waded into one, lifting me high so my cloak would not touch the water.

"The water hides our trail," he said once he'd crossed to the other side and resumed an easy run. Noting I was more awake, he asked, "Do ye remember the night we first took ye?"

"Yes."

We reached a small waterfall, and Erik did not slow. My

hand curled tighter around his neck, as he jumped down onto the rocks tumbled alongside the rushing water and kept going.

"Ye were such a wee thing, and so brave."

I blinked. The night the Berserkers came for us, Muriel and I had been asleep until they kicked in the door. My twin had risen up with a dagger in hand, while I cringed on the bed. A Berserker snatched her up easily, and Erik had closed in on me. I'd barely found enough breath to scream.

"Quiet, wee one," he'd crooned. "We won't hurt you."

"Please, leave me alone," I'd squeaked and cowered under a blanket. In a flash, he'd plucked me from the bed and carried me into the night air, much as he had last night.

Much as he carried me now.

"I wasn't brave."

"Ye were. We carried ye through the night, and though ye shivered, ye stayed awake and asked questions."

They'd stopped once to wrap me in a blanket of animal pelts. I'd met Gunnr then, and shrunk away from the large wolf form. He'd lain down and set his great head on his paws, keeping his mouth closed and acting as docile as a sheepdog. Eventually his gentleness lured me to pet him. The whole night had been strange beyond even one of my visions —starting with the frightening warriors bursting into our home, and ending with me seeking comfort from a giant black beast.

Erik seemed to be waiting for me to say something. "The stories you told were so fantastic. The witch's curse, the battles you won because of your Berserker rage--I almost didn't believe you were real."

"Do ye often see things that aren't real?" he asked with no judgment in his tone, but my gaze sharpened on his features. I'd learned young not to speak of things no one else could see. How would this Berserker react if I told him I'd had visions almost every moon? He might think me mad, and give me pity, or his beast might decide that I was dangerous. A mad wolf is a dead wolf. The pack might not tolerate someone so fey and touched by the gods. This Berserker might think the same, despite all the time we'd spent together.

I kept silent, but he didn't push me. As we journeyed on, I relaxed more and more in my captor's arms. Amusement danced over his full lips. His face, framed by a black beard, was comely despite a crooked nose that had surely been broken a few times.

He glanced up once, as the eagle soared across the empty blue sky. "Arne is jealous."

"What?"

"He wishes he was the one carrying ye." Erik gave me a toothy grin, made menacing by the sharp canines and gold glint his eyes. "He wishes us to stop soon, so he can take a turn. I told him he needs to keep to the sky."

"Why is Arne an eagle, when the rest of the Berserkers become wolves?"

"Let me ask him," Erik was silent a moment. "Arne tells me that he remembers little of the night the witch cursed us." A pause to grimace at his own memory of the night, and then the bearded warrior continued, "The witch slaughtered a wolf pack to feed the creature's flesh to us, but the magic in Arne's bloodline rejected it. When we all Changed into wolves, he took on the eagle's form."

I glanced at the sky; The eagle still spiraled in lazy loops above us. "When did he say that?"

"Just now."

"You can talk to him?"

"Sure. 'Tis the way the bond works. We can connect with the whole pack, but between my brothers the messages are clearer."

"Can't the Alphas speak to all wolves?"

"Aye." My grip tightened as Erik leaped from rock to rock. His hard muscled body absorbed the shock of each drop, so I barely felt it. "But we're blocking them and the pack bond right now."

"Why?"

"So they cannae track us. We're lone wolves. We've placed ourselves outside of the pack, and gone rogue."

"What does that mean?"

Erik's face now bore signs of strain. "We're now outsiders. If they catch us, we die."

AT DUSK, we detoured from the river to a deep forest grove. Erik didn't seem tired, even though he'd carried me in his arms and a small pack on his back for hours.

I'd dozed a little, and when the warrior let me down, I wobbled for a moment on stiff limbs. Body screaming for relief, I asked and Erik allowed me to go behind some bushes for a moment's privacy.

When I returned Erik had already dragged some dead limbs into a pile. Arne had arrived, a swift shadow moving through the woods, helped Erik build up a fire.

Gunnr pushed out of the thicket, a bird carcass in his jaws. He dropped it near the fire and came to me.

He sniffed me over while I stroked the thick fur of his back and fondled his soft ears.

"I'm all right," I told him. "Just tired." I curled into him, the events of last night and today hitting me like a weight. Even though Erik had carried me, I felt like I'd run all day.

Arne left his work long enough to drape a blanket made of pelts over me. "Rest little one."

"How much farther are we going?" I yawned and laid my head on Gunnr's back.

"No farther. Tonight, we stay here."

The wolf turned his head and licked my cheek. I wanted to ask why these warriors had taken me, what they expected me to do for them. They'd risked everything to take me because they believed I was their mate. What if they were wrong?

I woke to Erik's hand on my shoulder. "Come, lass. Ye need to eat."

Gunnr had curled around me, supporting me with his warm weight. I sat up slowly, and thanked Erik when he brought me a piece of meat and tucked the cloak tighter around me.

He sat on a rock nearby, watching me eat. When I was done, I fed the wolf the leftover bones.

I sank back against him with a sigh.

"Now Arne and I are both jealous."

"Why?"

"Because Gunnr gets to sleep with ye."

I frowned. It was easy for me to forget Gunnr was really a man. The wolf bared his teeth in a semblance of a grin, and bent his head to crunch the rest of the bones.

"He wishes he were not bound to his wolf form. He wants to hold you in his arms."

"Why is he always a wolf?" I asked.

"Gunnr was the strongest of us, and helped us control our beasts. Over time, this weakened him and he was overcome. Changing into a wolf keeps him from losing himself to the Berserker bond."

Gunnr gazed at me, so much intelligence in the animal face. There were a few white hairs on his muzzle, the only marking on his midnight coat. What did he look like as a man? Would I ever know?

He'd be gone forever if the beast consumed his mind.

"How is the wolf different than the beast?" I asked Erik, rubbing Gunnr's giant paw.

"The wolf is natural magic. There are werewolves who are simply men and wolf. They live in harmony with their nature. When the witch cursed us, she made us wolves, but with more power. The beast is part of the curse, the tainted magic."

My shoulders heaved with my sigh. I wrapped the cloak tight around me.

Gunnr whined at the loss of my touch.

"What's wrong, lass?"

"It's nothing."

"Tell us your thoughts," Arne seated himself nearby. "We do not want you to fear us. When we are mated there will be no secrets between us."

I bit my lip. They'd risked so much, claiming me despite the pack trying to keep us apart. Perhaps I could risk a little as well.

"Is there any magic that is not a curse?" The warriors didn't seem surprised at my outburst, but their bodies tensed as if they were ready to go to battle for me.

"I have magic," I continued. "I wish I did not. I'd cut it out of me if I could." It had made me sick my entire life, filled my days with waking nightmares. I saw things I should not see. "It is evil."

"It is a gift," Arne shook his head. "The goddess gifted you with the Sight. You would be prized in the Northlands as a seer. A vala, or witch woman."

"Ye have great power, Fleur," Erik added.

"Power? My power only weakens me."

"We believe we can help," Arne said.

"How?"

"As the mating bond forms, we will support the weight of your Sight. Just as the three of us are able to fight the grip of the Berserker rage, we will give you respite from your abilities."

"We can help ye, Fleur. Ye are not alone."

They looked so excited and eager, but I only felt tired.

"It sounds too good to be true." I let my head fall back on Gunnr's body and closed my eyes.

Gunnr's soothing warmth and Erik's voice followed me into my dreams.

"Dinnae worry, lass. We'll get you well."

THE NEXT TIME I WOKE, Erik was bending over me, bowl in hand. I sat up and he held it for me as I drank the rich broth. When my mouth moistened enough to be able to speak, I thanked him.

"It is good. When did you make it?"

"We've been here a day and night."

"I slept that long?" The clearing was empty but for Erik and a low fire. The wolf and Arne were gone.

"Aye, and you're looking better. How do you feel?" He stroked the hair back from my face.

I stretched out my arms as a test. "I'm well." The stiffness in my body was banished by my long rest. "Hungry."

"Finish the broth then," he said, looking pleased. "Once that's settled we'll give ye some honey cakes."

Under Erik's careful watch, I ate slowly but steadily. The large tattooed warrior kept playing nursemaid, building up the fire to make more broth, tucking the blanket around my legs, even kneeling behind me to braid my hair back. I submitted to his touch as if he was one of my sisters. A few days and these warriors had already accustomed me to their claim. After stoking up the fire, Erik didn't leave my side.

When I was finished, he took the bowl. I started to rise, and he laid a hand on my chest.

"Go slowly, lass."

His big hand splayed just above my breasts. I felt the heat of it through my thin shift, and flushed, feeling less like an invalid and more like a woman.

"Please, I feel much better. I need to relieve myself."

He helped me totter to the bushes, and gave me some privacy, though he hovered close.

I did my business and walked with more strength back to the fire, with Erik dogging my steps. I wobbled once and it was enough for him to scoop me up again.

"I thought this illness had ended," I grumbled to distract me from how much I liked being in his arms. He seemed to take every opportunity to touch me.

"Arne thinks the exhaustion came upon ye because of the long journey and your worries. Dinnae worry, lass. You'll become stronger, especially now that you're with us."

I wanted to argue but couldn't deny how much better I felt, and how nice it was to be coddled and cared for by the burly warriors.

Erik set me on a stone to sip more broth as he worked around the camp.

"Any word from the pack?" I asked.

"They're angry. We've cut ourselves off from them. " He passed a hand over his forehead, frowning a little, but the grimace disappeared by the time he returned to my side.

"Any chance they will find us here?"

"No chance. Arne placed protection over the camp. Not even a witch can find us."

He took the empty bowl and held out his hand. "Come, lass. Let us visit the river."

Strength returned to me as I walked beside him, my arm tucked into the crook of his tattooed one. The sound of rushing water grew louder, and Gunnr slipped out of the forest to pad silently behind us.

I stopped to greet the black wolf.

"Thank you for guarding me as I slept," I whispered to him. "My dreams were good because of you."

The wolf grinned, tongue lolling out.

"This way, lass," Erik called. He too, wore a big smile.

I lifted my skirts to walk the rest of the way. The Northman let me make my own path, though he still hovered. With little brushes of a hand on my shoulder, a nudge on my hip, he propelled me to where he wanted me to go.

As we grew closer to the river, Erik detoured and led me to a woodland pool. He motioned to the water, shimmering and still in the heat of the day.

"I thought you might wish to wash."

After removing my boots, I lifted the hem of my shift up to my knees to wade into the pool.

Erik caught my arm.

"You dinnae wish to strip naked?"

"No." I frowned at the ground.

"You should get used to being naked around us," he said, but did not make me take off my shift.

It needed cleaning anyway.

I entered the water, arms crossed over the thin fabric. The garment would be practically see through when it was wet. My heart beat faster at the thought of these warriors seeing my bare form, but I scolded that thought right away. No one wanted a scrawny, sickly girl. These warriors had seen me at my worst, and wanted me as a mate, but they did not truly desire me.

At least that was what I told myself over and over, until I heard a splash behind me.

Erik waded through the water after me, his pale chest on display in all its glory of scars and corded muscles.

The very water seemed to heat around me and though I was not naked, I dipped quickly, feeling exposed. Erik swam around me in slow circles, grinning all the while.

I pretended to ignore him.

The day was warm and fine, and the black wolf slept on the sunny bank. The water refreshed my sleepy body as I scrubbed my skin. There was no soap or herbs for cleaning, but I did my best, pulling frustrated fingers through my tangled hair.

Distracted, I backed into a warm wall.

"Allow me," Erik murmured in my ear.

His large hand squeezed my neck, a light reminder of his power. I bowed my head as his fingers slipped through my fair locks, massaging my scalp until my body melted.

"I did not know Berserkers could do such gentle things."

"I find I am learning to do all manner of things I did not know were possible, for you."

I sighed and leaned against his hard chest, my cheek just

inches away from sculpted muscle. The water ran in rivulets down the plains and valleys of his broad torso.

I licked my lips.

"Thirsty, lass?"

Shaking my head as if dazed, I swam away.

Grinning ear to ear, Erik sank into the water, and surged back up, flinging water from his black hair. His head was dark and shiny as a raven's.

The warrior began swimming around me again, a smirk on his face.

My throat suddenly dry, I swallowed several times before I could speak. "You are a Berserker. From the Northland, yes?"

"Yes. Vikings, they called us."

"Yet you do not have their fair hair." I pointed out.

"No, wee flower." He swam nearer. "My mother was a slave, as was Arne's. We won our freedom by fighting for the jarl in our homeland. Joined with the group of warriors who went to the witch, and there we were cursed as Berserkers."

He moved into my space, so close his chest nearly brushed mine. My nipples hardened beneath the wet drape of my shift.

I swallowed hard and took a step back towards the shore. He followed me, tilting his head as if daring me to run. It would be a short chase. The gold in his eyes told me his beast was close to the surface.

My heart beat like the wings of a frightened bird, but I wasn't scared of him. I didn't know what I felt.

"I'm sorry the witch cursed you."

"I'm not." He kept crowding me. "It brought me to ye."

When I turned from him, his fingers slipped over my bare shoulder. He lifted the wet hair from my neck and his mouth descended, sucking water from my skin.

My body caught fire.

"Erik," I gasped.

"Say my name," he murmured against my neck.

Knees weak, I barely found the strength to step away. "You cannot do this."

"Why not?"

I bit my lip before I could argue that he didn't really want me. Whatever my frail charms, they were enough to arouse his beast.

"Dinnae deny the pull between us. Wherever our feelings lead, you want it; I want it."

"I don't want it." My breasts and my cunny tingled, making a liar out of me. "Please, this is not right. I am supposed to choose a mate."

"We told you. We made the decision. Ye belong to us."

"What will the pack say?"

"The pack isnae here." He shrugged. "Admit it. Ye are relieved. Ye wanted to choose us."

"I would've chosen you. But they would not allow it."

"Did they tell ye why?"

The black wolf still lay on the bank, his eyes closed. "Gunnr," I lowered my voice. "The Alphas feared for my safety if I took you three as mate. Erik—is it true? Did he attack Sabine?"

"He did, but he is better now."

Catching my hand, Erik drew me further into the pool. We swam in a lazy spiral. Every so often he pulled me closer, and I took every opportunity to stretch further away. We moved in that private dance until he tugged me into his arms.

His teeth nipped at my shoulder and a shiver threatened to unhinge my spine.

"Ye want us. Soon you will admit it," he whispered.

I was about to agree when a whine caught my ears. Gunnr waited on the edge of the bank, giant black paws half in the water.

"Erik." I nudged the black-haired warrior.

The Norseman sighed and backed away. "Come. We will get ye dressed."

4

Anew, fur-lined pair of boots and a heavy brocade overdress waited on a sunny rock.

I lifted it in awe at the weight of the fabric and detail of the stitches. "This is a dress for a lady."

"Nothing but the best for our captive Berserker bride." Erik winked at me.

My shift dried quickly in the midday sun. Erik helped me into the gunna, and tied back my hair.

"Lovely," Arne called. He'd returned from his scouting and now leaned against a tree, Gunnr at his side. "Ready to eat, little flower? Gunnr brought us a roast boar."

Back at our camp, I devoured the food and tossed my bones to Gunnr. The warriors waited until I'd eaten my fill, then fell on the carcass, tearing it apart with their hands, ripping the meat off the bone with ultra sharp canines.

I sat on a rock, weaving a braid out of flowers. Dressed in leather breeches and nothing else, Erik and Arne looked like wild men. Their sleek muscles gleamed in the firelight.

When their meal was done, they stretched out near me like contented wolves. Erik let out a belch. Arne grinned and released a louder one. Not to be outdone, they both filled the night with burping sounds.

I threw the floral wreath down and they paused to look at me. "Now what?"

"What do you mean, Fleur?" Arne asked.

"You've taken me from the pack. We're on the run. Eventually the pack will hunt us down. So what is your plan?"

"Do we need one?"

I stared at the Moor as if he'd sprouted horns. "You snatched a potential bride away from the entire pack. The Alphas will have no choice to but to order your deaths."

Erik came and seated himself beside me. His hand circled my ankle, a simple but intimate gesture. His thumb stroked my skin.

"Will ye admit ye are mated to us?"

"Yes, gladly, if it will save your lives."

Arne arched a brow. "You would do that for us? Just to save us from the Alphas' wrath?"

"Of course. I'll tell them I convinced you to help me run away."

The warrior's exchanged glances.

"'Tis a good plan, and for that we thank ye. But your tale will not be enough to convince the pack."

"I don't know what else to say."

Erik's thumb kept teasing my skin. "It wouldn't be a lie to say that we took ye because ye are our true mate."

"But I'm not," I said.

"Are you so sure?" Arne asked.

I had nothing to say to that, unless I wanted to admit the vision of me in the tomb.

"There is a way to convince the pack that you're our mate, and we were meant to claim ye."

"Oh?" I asked. "And what's that?"

Arne cleared his throat. "We must work on the bond."

"Bond?"

"Aye, lass. Do ye know how the mating process works?"

I flushed. "My sisters explained some things to me. I watched rabbits, um, mate in the wild."

"Rabbits," the warriors chortled. "We are not rabbits."

"No, you are not," I murmured as their laughter rippled the beautiful muscles of their chests and throats.

"There are three things required for werewolves to mate." Arne ticked them off on his fingers. "Mating bite, mating heat, mating bond."

"I am not a werewolf."

"No, but like your sisters, ye have your own form of magic."

"Spaewives are blessed with a natural magic. They are perfect werewolf brides. They can go into heat."

"The mating heat is a sign that you are primed and ready to be taken to mate."

I bit my lip, thinking of the warmth that spread through my body now when the warriors touched me. It was getting harder and harder to ignore.

Three pairs of glowing eyes fixed on me, as if reading my thoughts.

"So how does the bond form?" I started in alarm when Arne rose and stalked to sit opposite Erik on the other side of me. Pressing my legs together, I held back a slight shiver, and responding quiver in my cunny.

Erik teased a lock of my hair. "Do ye trust us lass?"

"I barely know you," I whispered.

"That does not matter," Arne murmured, tracing the neckline of my gown. His touch made my skin pebble, but not with cold. "Would you like to get to know us?"

On my left, Erik ran his finger along my dress, and hooked the fabric to tug it off my shoulder.

"What are you doing?" My heart flipped.

Arne laid a large hand on my neck, drawing my attention back to him.

"Relax, little blossom." Pulling me closer, he studied me for a moment before he touched his lips to mine.

Erik's mouth touched the bare skin of my left shoulder at the same time.

Warmth poured through me at the mere brush of their lips. It lasted but a moment, but left me undone, blinking in surprise and wonder at the sensations flooding my body.

"Nervous, wee one?"

"I-that was—"

Arne's large hand massaged my neck, strong fingers soothing my vulnerable flesh, forcing me to relax.

Erik's hands combed through my hair, lifting it away from my ear. "Did ye like your kiss?"

"We'll know if you lie to us," Arne reminded.

"It felt nice. Um, do the two of you, both..."

"When we claim a mate we will take her together."

"How is that possible?" My sister had explained some of this to me, but I'd forgotten. I'd never thought I'd need to know how to please two men.

"We'll teach ye that, when it is time."

A slight sigh escaped me, a little sound of wanting.

The warrior's eyes lit as soon as they heard it, the predators within them sensing their prey was near, and weak.

Rearing up, I broke away from them, fleeing a few paces towards the fire. "I can't do this," I said.

I made sure my body didn't tremble before I turned to face them. They waited on the log, faces impassive. No anger or disappointment at my outburst.

"Very well, Fleur," Arne said. "Why don't you get some rest?"

"Now?" The sun had past its zenith but still rode high in the sky.

"'Tis hot," Erik shrugged. "Arne has placed wards around our camp. We are safe, for now. Are ye not sleepy?"

I caught a hint of amusement in his voice.

"No...I could sleep." I skirted the fire to the bedroll, keeping as much distance between me and the men. The events of the day hadn't worn me out but my limbs were still weak and recovering. It would give me a chance to regroup my strength, so I could resist these men. I hadn't thought my body would betray me.

But when I lay down, no matter how I curled up on the blanket, I couldn't get comfortable.

My body was too hot for clothes.

My lower lips throbbed, heavy and swollen under my gown. My nipples pressed against the fabric. Whatever was happening in my body, sleep would be impossible.

Erik leaned over me, propping his rolled jerkin under my head as a pillow. The leather held the scent of him.

"If the heat of the day is too much, ye can take off your heavy dress, if ye wish."

He winked at me and sat down.

I shrank to one side of the bedroll, afraid if I touched him I might combust. The heat of the day was nothing compared to the slow burn in my body, centered between my legs.

"Are you sleeping here too?"

He paused. "Would ye prefer it if I Change into a wolf?"

"No. Do as you wish." I rolled to my side facing away from him. A slight wind lifted my hair and ran a shiver down my back.

When I looked back, a brown wolf with black markings sat gazing at me.

"Erik?"

"He thinks you will cuddle him as you do Gunnr if he's in wolf form." Arne sat down next to me, his hip bumping mine. I sat up in protest, and he scooted closer, pushing me to the middle of the bedroll so his big body could take one half. Arne threaded an arm around me, drawing me to the bedrolls while the wolves trotted away.

"Erik and Gunnr will guard the perimeter. I told them it is time for you to learn to lie next to your mates in man form. Don't worry, Fleur," he grinned. "We will only sleep. Truth is, I need the rest."

My heart beat faster. I had dreamed of lying in this warrior's arms, and now it was coming to pass. My entire body came alive, tingles centering on the place between my legs. My cunny throbbed. I'd never felt this way before. Part of me wanted to run and hide so I could examine my body and reassure myself that I was still Fleur, thin and frail young, possessing none of the glowing beauty my sisters had. Another part wanted to throw myself into Arne's ready arms, and let him wake more of the latent passion threatening to consume me.

The warrior smiled as if he knew my feelings, and that I was fighting them. I let him pull me back down, but again rolled to my side facing away from him, careful that our bodies did not touch.

Chuckling, he pulled me to him, my back to his front. His touch seared my skin and I hid my gasp.

"What are you doing?" I asked as soon as I could speak without panting.

Tucking me closer against his bare chest, he draped a leg over mine, and slipped his arm tighter around my waist.

"What I've wanted to do since I met you. Hush now, and rest. You are still recovering."

He kissed the back of my neck, the tender spot that made my body liquid.

I'd never had a man hold me like this. My sisters might have men lust after them, but I'd never been beautiful and desired.

Until now.

I waited until his breathing evened out.

"I've dreamed of you holding me like this," I whispered. "Ever since you came and healed me."

"I know, little flower." I startled when Arne spoke. His deep voice wasn't sleepy at all. "Those were the nights I imagined you in my arms."

My hand sought his where it splayed over my midriff. The desire in his tone made me bold. "I never knew you wanted me."

He raised himself up, frowning down at me. "Truly?"

"I am not pretty like my sisters, and I am always sick."

"Your sickness is really an evil spirit attacking you."

I rolled to my back to face him. "What?"

"I have been studying it. As an eagle I fly high over the earth, and I have a little of the Sight because of my ancestor's power. From what I can tell, the evil stems from a cave in a barren, desolate place."

"You see the Grey Men too?"

"Not exactly. What you see as 'Grey Men' are really an extension of the evil of those two places. They look like people, to most men's eyes. Your Sight allows you to see their decaying soul."

If I wasn't lying in the shelter of Arne's big body, totally protected, I wouldn't have the courage to speak on this subject. "What are they?" I asked in a hushed tone, as if the evil Arne spoke of might be nearby and listening.

"They are not people, they are not spirits. My guess is they are a body of a person sacrificed to an evil purpose, their souls are enslaved, and they are controlled by a greater power, someone with enough magic to create this army of half dead servants."

I gulped. "A greater evil?"

"Yes. Whatever creature controls the Grey Men has the power beyond a witch or warlock. The magic is tainted beyond any I've ever known. It is sorcery."

A chill went through me, despite being pressed against Arne's warm body. A witch might gather power by sacrifice: a bit of human blood spilled, or the slaughter of a rabbit or a small bird. The larger the kill, the more powerful, and darker the magic. What sort of sacrifice did this sorcerer's magic require?

Arne toyed with a lock of my hair. "My guess is the sorcerer's servant found you in the market and tried to subdue you so he could carry you back to his creator. The curse stayed with you until my talisman dispelled it."

A curse explained why I had made such a rapid recovery.

"But I've had fevers and sickness all my life."

"When did you start seeing the Grey Men?"

I was young and playing on the edge of the market where my mother had a stall. When I pointed out the grim creature, my mother had hushed me. I'd learned to keep silent about the things I saw. Other than Muriel, no one knew the extent of my Sight.

After that Seeing, the fevers began.

"Yes," Arne said when I told him. "The fevers awakened

with your power. You felt the oppressiveness of their presence, and battled it, without knowing what you did."

"Until this last time, the Grey Men never noticed me.
Something must have changed."

"Aye, Fleur. You."

Arne lay back down and slid his arm around my middle
again. This time, he held my wrist in a reassuring, dominant
grip. "You've changed since you've come to the Berserkers.
You've grown from a girl into a lovely young woman." I held
my breath as his thumb played with the soft skin of my
inner wrist. Could he tell the moment my pulse picked up?

"I don't think that's it..."

"No?" His mouth was so close to my ear, his lips caressed
the outer edge. "Tomorrow we will show you just how lovely
we think you are."

"I didn't mean..." His teeth tugged at my earlobe and I
fought to rally my thoughts. "I know I am desired by the
pack as a mate."

"Mmmm," Arne's tongue touched a sensitive spot on my
neck and a shudder ran through me.

"What I wanted to say was...I think the pack magic kept
the Grey Men away."

"Yes." Arne's mouth left my skin. "And now my warrior
brothers and I will see to your protection."

"But—"

Gripping my wrist, Arne moved my hand and pressed it
at the apex of my legs. I gasped as heat pooled under my
palm, red hot desire flowing from every part of me to my
throbbing core.

What had I been arguing about?

"Like it or not, we are your mates. We will prove this to
you as well. The three of us have pledged ourselves to you.

Above all, we will keep you safe, and you will thrive in our care."

He moved my hand and the ache between my legs eased. His words sank in like a brand on my soul.

"Sleep now." There was a command in his voice, a soporific, weighting my eyes. Alphas could command the pack with just a word. The Berserker holding me in his arms had this power over me—I should've been afraid of him, afraid of the evil he described, but instead I felt safe. With every passing day, these warriors drove themselves deeper into my heart.

I had one more sleepy thought.

"Arne? The Alphas said I couldn't choose you because Gunnr is unstable. But you're strong, right? You're not going to lose control."

He paused so long, I wondered if he had heard me.

"Arne?"

"Let us worry about controlling our beast. You focus on getting well, and accepting us as your mates."

I DREAMT I swam in a warm, languid river, and when I woke the throbbing between my legs had increased tenfold.

Arne's hand lifted the hair from my neck; he kissed it lightly, a gesture that made me shiver with happiness.

"How long did I sleep?"

"Long enough."

I came awake. Arne was behind me, naked but for a loin-cloth around his nethers. The warrior lay bare and willing right next to me. It was not a dream.

I rolled to face the large warrior stretched out beside me.

"Are you all right, Fleur?"

"I've never felt this way before." My forehead burned, feverish, but instead of weakness, my body hummed with energy. "Something's wrong with me."

"Nothing's wrong." He stroked my flaxen hair away from my face.

"What is happening?"

"'Tis your heat." His eyes burned gold.

I lay a hand on Arne's taut chest. I wanted to trace his muscles, pour wine down the bronze plate of his torso and lick him clean.

"I want..." I licked my lips, imagining everything I would do to him.

"What do you want?"

He caught my wrists, pulling me to straddle him. My body was so slight next to his strong one, he easily maneuvered me into position seated on his taut stomach, and lay back, smiling.

I sighed. With my legs on either side of his body, my pulsing cunny pressed right on the hard ridges of his muscled abdomen. The ache between my legs grew and I started rolling my hips, finding the friction I needed to sate it.

"Yes." He growled as I rubbed against him.

My nipples hardened to points.

I rocked faster.

"Please," I begged him, though I didn't know why.

"That's it, little flower. Use me as you will. Find your pleasure."

I set my hand against his great chest, my pale fingers against his dusky skin. His muscles flexed and rippled as if he fought to hold still, but he lay quietly, his hands hovering at my hips, ready to steady me, as he watched me with an impassioned look.

"Arne," I breathed his name. He was so beautiful. I wanted to bend down fully and press my lips to his, but I could not bear to stop rocking against him.

"That's it." His eyes crinkled. His length grew against my bottom. I'd caught glimpses of its size through the loincloth he always wore right after the Change. How would it feel inside me? I'd never wondered such a thing before, but now the thoughts boiled through me, cascades of flame licking through my limbs. I didn't even notice that my shift had ridden up, baring my lower half, until Arne's hand slipped under my dress, gliding up over my stomach to cup one of my breasts. His large hand caressed my sensitive flesh. My back arched, pressing further into his touch.

Something inside me snapped and warmth poured through my body, a flood centering on the apex of my thighs.

I rode my climax, little pants and cries escaping my lax mouth.

Arne watched the whole thing, his eyes burning me, but not once did I look away. His hands came to my hips, steadying me.

As soon as I found my balance, his right hand slid back to splay against my bare stomach, just under the thin shift.

"That was," he paused in awe, his deep voice rumbling through the very core of me, "the most beautiful thing I've ever seen."

I smiled and leaned my weight on him until my hand slipped a little. There was wet on his chest where my lower lips touched him.

With a gasp, I scrambled to my feet. I'd behaved like a wanton.

"Fleur?" Arne rose, concern creasing his brow.

Sticky hand raised to ward him off, I backed away. "What was that? What have I done?"

"You gave into your desires. That was natural, and right."

"It was wrong. I shouldn't have done it."

"Talk to me, Fleur," Arne soothed. "Tell me your fears."

"This wasn't supposed to happen. This isn't my destiny." I had seen my death, and accepted it. I could not fall in love. "I took advantage of you. I am sorry."

"Easy, easy. You did nothing that I did not allow. Do you really think I couldn't stop you if I wished to?" His gentle teasing broke down another wall. I let out a nervous laugh and kept backing away. These men were more dangerous than I'd realized. My foolish body was all too willing to betray me, yet again.

I whirled to run, and tattooed arms caught me. "Oh no, wee one," Erik said. "Ye will not flee from us now."

My struggle came to naught. Wrapped in his arms, I sagged against his strong form. "I cannot be this way."

"Why not?" Arne asked.

"Do ye not want us?"

"It doesn't matter. I cannot do this." I fought again and Erik let me down. Instead of running, I grabbed up the fur cloak and wrapped myself in it. "I don't want you to see me like this."

"What?" Arne said, just as Erik pressed, "Why ever not?"

My cheeks flushed in humiliation at having to explain it. "Because I am ugly. I am too thin and frail."

"Ye jest," Erik growled.

Arne held up a hand, signaling his warrior brother to calm down. "Tell us, Fleur."

"I am not like my sisters." They were all strong and lovely in their own way. "I am not beautiful, or worthy to be a Berserker bride." *And I will not survive the year.* I tucked that thought away, deep. I would never admit that to these men, and destroy their hope. I cared for them too much, despite fighting against my feelings. Better to drive them away so they abandoned me before I died.

"Fleur, do you truly believe you aren't beautiful?" Arne asked.

"I cannae believe it." Erik seemed angry, as if someone had insulted him. "We would risk our lives at a chance to possess ye--"

"We already have," Arne broke in.

"And ye don't think you're worthy."

The black-haired warrior stalked closer, too quickly for me to flee. Rough hands caught my face, his touch gentle. "Can ye be serious?"

I didn't dare respond.

His fingers stroked along my jawline.

"A light shines in your eyes. Your cheeks are pink with health."

Arne's hands settled above my hips. "Your waist tight, small enough for me to span with my hands."

Erik slid fingers down my neck and shoulders. "Ye have a comely shape. Your body, your breasts," his eyes dropped lower, "I have not even seen ye, but I want to."

My legs wobbled. Erik caught me up in his arms.

"Please, you should not touch me," I protested, even as my insides clenched with delicious anticipation.

A deep growl silenced me. I no longer spoke with Erik the man, but the beast within, wild and untamed. Arne stalked after us, the same feral look in his eye. My skin tingled. Was it possible that they truly desired me?

They carried me back to the woodland pool. A shadow

darted through the trees, but the midnight wolf did not appear.

"Is that Gunnr?" I asked.

"Yes," Arne said. "But until he is a man, he will not take part in this."

"In what?" I asked as Erik stopped right at the edge and set me down to tug my cloak away.

"What are you doing?"

"What I should've done from the first." In a whoosh, he'd stripped me of my light shift. I crossed my arms over my body, and Erik forced my hands down gently.

My pale body was fully on display. Small breasts, a narrow waist flaring out to my hips and bottom. Golden down hid my nether lips. My legs were lean but firm with muscle.

Part of me was excited. Part of me wanted them to see me, all of me. I'd felt so strong and lovely, riding Arne to climax. Perhaps I could have another taste of pleasure, just once, before I had to push these men away again.

The warriors stared at me so long I grew nervous all over again.

Erik lifted his hand as if to touch me but only brushed a skein of hair behind my shoulder. "This is what ye seek to hide from us?"

I nodded.

Gold lit his eyes.

"I would risk death a thousand times just for a chance to hold ye."

"Isn't that just the magic between us? My abilities soothing your curse?"

"We won't lie and say we don't want you for that. But we are also men. And you are the woman we desire."

"Here, lass. We'll prove it to you."

Arne laid the fur cloak down on a large, flat rock, and Erik set me on it.

They handed me a bowl of water, a vial of oil, and a blade.

"What's this?"

Both men squatted close, stripped down to their loincloths.

"We want to see ye," Erik said.

"See me?"

"Aye. All of ye." He pointed. "We wish ye to be bare between your legs."

"Fleur, we want you to shave. We're going to watch."

"What?"

"If ye won't do it, I will," Erik growled and started to rise. Arne caught his arm.

"No, no, I'll do it," I said. Though I wasn't sure I could with them crouching close, their golden gaze devouring my flesh.

Lifting the blade, I forced my hand steady.

"Part your legs." I did so and they both leaned forward.

"Wider, lass."

Feet spread flat on the rock, I slathered the oil over my lower lips.

With careful strokes I shaved away the blonde down. At the end, my labia were bare and shining with the oil.

"Lie back," Arne commanded.

I flinched when they moved to sit on either side of me. "What are you doing?"

"Shhh, be still. We will not hurt ye." One bronze hand, one tattooed ghosted over my flesh, raising goosebumps at the promise of their touch.

"Put your hands over your head and keep them there. If you move them, we will tie you up. Understand?"

I nodded.

Instead of fingers, a feather touched me. Arne traced my collarbone with it.

"You still have the feather I gave you."

"Yes, I kept it," I breathed. His smile was my reward.

Something tickled my side. Erik ran a flower along the curve of my waist and swirled it up to dance under my bare breasts.

"Close your eyes, lass. Let us enjoy ye."

The flower and feather danced over my skin. Every so often a tremor went through me, beginning and ending at my pulsing core.

"Reach down and part your lower lips," Erik ordered.

I sighed as my fingers spread the plump folds. My labia was warm and swollen.

"Your sweetness gushes out at the lightest touch," Arne growled.

"Here, lass. Taste it."

The flower brushed my mouth, smearing my juices on my lips before dipping between my legs again.

My knees jerked closer together.

"Keep your legs open, wee flower, or we'll tie them apart."

"That would be a pleasing sight. Winding the ropes around her limbs, tying the ends to trees, stretching her arms and legs. Keeping her bound and helpless, waiting for us."

I gasped. His words struck a blaze that raged through me. The muscles at my core tightened, aching for release just out of reach.

The feather brushed my breasts, the flower pressed between my legs.

Just when I couldn't take it any more, they both went away.

I opened my eyes.

"I'm going to use this to enter you," Arne held up a wooden cylinder narrowed to a point on one end, gleaming with oil. "It will break the barrier of skin at your entrance. It will hurt a little, but then we will give you great pleasure."

I nodded.

"Can you keep your legs apart for me or do you wish Erik to help you?"

I blinked at Erik's handsome face. "Please help me."

"I will, lass." Instead of holding me down, as I expected, he leaned over me. His lips found mine, his beard tickling my mouth.

Arne sat between my legs and the wooden piece entered me. In a swift movement it tore through something inside me with a little pain.

The little twinge was nothing compared to the wanton throbbing between my legs.

"How was that, Fleur?"

"Mmmm," I hummed happily against Erik's lips. "More."

"Good." Arne chuckled. "And now the pleasure."

Erik sat back up. Took a nipple between a finger and thumb and tugged lightly.

I squirmed but did nothing to stop him.

"Do that again," Arne said. "She liked it. Her cunny gushes with honey."

Before I could close my legs, the big warrior took hold of my knees and pushed my legs even wider.

"Your body parts like a flower for me. So lovely and ready. I'm going to use my fingers to give you pleasure."

"Yes, please," I breathed.

Arne played with my pink petals, his expert touches stoking the flames at my core higher and higher.

Erik thumbed my nipple and it became too much.

Pleasure broke over me in small, lulling waves. My hips rocked involuntarily.

"Yes. That's it, wee one. Take your pleasure."

My climax still tingled through me when the men took their hands away. "What was that?"

Arne grinned at me.

"The beginning."

5

After that, it was no use fighting their touches. Instead of a dress, the warriors draped the cloak over my shoulders and I wore it around the camp as they roasted more meat.

From time to time, Arne or Erik would tug me close and draw open the fur covering to gaze on my naked flesh. Their looks heated me further until I was leaning into them, almost begging them to touch me.

When night fell, Erik sat me on his lap and fed me by hand. I licked his fingers while Arne gazed at us across the fire, drinking mead.

'Go to him,' Erik ordered. I rose and he tugged at the robe. "Naked."

Drunk on their pleasure and mine, I let it fall and walked slowly to the warrior, moving my hips seductively. Firelight licked at my bare flesh, molding it with gilt and shadow.

When I stood in front of him, Arne offered the skein. "Do you want some mead, little blossom?"

Biting my lip, I nodded.

Slinging a pelt at his feet, he motioned to it. "Then kneel."

I did, my hands on his muscled legs. I couldn't help my gaze flicking to the bulge in his leather breeches.

He held the skein to my lips. "Drink."

I kept my hands on his knees and accepted what he tipped into my mouth, licking my lips after swallowing the mouthful. His great chest rose and fell faster.

"My turn," Erik called.

I rose and took the skein, when I turned, Arne's hands cupped the curve of my bottom.

I smiled to encourage him.

Erik's canines shone white in the firelight. He pointed to the ground between his feet. "The same as you were with Arne."

I knelt and lifted the skein to him, watched the strong line of his neck swallow as he drank.

He set it to my lips and I drank. Arne took the skein for another swallow. This time he leaned forward and kissed me, tasting of mead and man. I laid my hands along the stubbled plane of his jaw, crushing my mouth against his as the liquid poured into my mouth.

When he drew away, I kept my hands where they were. "Again."

"Greedy one." He kissed me again, without the mead, and I twined my arms around his neck, half in his lap, half out, wholly consumed by the pleasure of his mouth.

My chest rose and fell rapidly when our lips parted.

"I feel hot," I told him. Taking his large hand, I slid it down my bare body and pressed it between my legs. His fingers stroked me and I arched back, hands on his shoulders, pushing further into his touch.

"Fleur—" A pained look crossed Erik's face. Before he

could move, I straddled him, grinding down on the thick length of his cock, hard and ready under his breeches. I'd seen two villagers in secret tryst and wondered at the frantic writhing of their bodies. I understood now. The heat claimed my mind and all I could think about was rubbing myself to satiety.

Arne was behind me suddenly, wrapping me in the fur cloak, lifting me up.

"Not yet, little flower."

A whimper broke from me. I struggled and he turned me to face him.

"I want it," I begged. "I want you."

"We know, little Fleur. Not tonight, when you are gone with drink."

I slid down his broad chest, clawing at his great muscles. "Please, I am aching for you."

"Fleur," Erik's arms captured me from behind. "Be still."

"No," I cried.

"We will take ye soon, I promise," he whispered furiously. "But not until ye are ready."

"I am ready. I want you."

"You are young, and fragile."

I kicked at him, a roar breaking from me. The pressure between my legs was unbearable, it filled me with a want that made my head throb. I became a wild thing.

Erik lifted me easily and lay me down on the bedroll. He held me down, pinning my wrists above my head, weighting me with his body.

I fought as much as I could and didn't move an inch. He waited until I stopped thrashing and went limp under him.

"Will ye mind?"

My head rested on the ground. The insistent pressure had passed.

"Yes. I am better now."

He let me up but pulled me into his lap much as I had been earlier. This time, he held my wrists behind me.

"You will obey us. We will satisfy your every desire, but not until we all are ready."

"Forgive me," I whispered.

"There's nothing to forgive. We want you, Fleur, have no doubt about that, but we must go slowly or risk losing control."

"I know. I don't know what that was. I don't know what came over me."

"'Twas your heat." Erik released my arms, and I wrapped them around myself, miserable.

Arne squatted close to us. "Don't be ashamed. This is a good sign."

"My body is not my own," I said to the ground.

"No. It is ours, and we will handle you with care," Arne said, and Erik gently pried my arms open. Both men lay down with me on my side between them. I faced the Moor.

"When we take you, Fleur, you will know beyond a doubt that you belong to us."

Beyond him, Gunnr's black wolf edged from the trees, watching us. I'd spent every night with him since his warrior brothers had claimed me but things had changed. I was a new woman, come into my own desires. The warriors had made me ready and eager for our future mating, and I would sleep between them, a woman with her lovers.

There was no longer a place for the wolf.

"Sleep now." Erik tucked me closer to his body. Arne captured my hand and held it against his chest before closing his eyes.

Gunnr loped away.

I SLEPT SOUNDLY between my two warriors, and woke when I was lifted into someone's arms.

"What-?"

"Keep quiet, wee one," Erik whispered. "Arne has spotted a party of Berserkers. The pack is coming closer to finding us, so we are on the move."

That brought me wide awake. He ran, carrying me bundled in the fur cloak, and Gunnr ran alongside. We met Arne at the bank of a stream.

"They lost the trail," he reported, "but may soon find it again. I left false traces of a camp a league south of here."

"We must find another place to settle," Erik said, frowning. "All this moving is hard on our mate."

I almost protested that I was strong enough to keep up, but it would have been of no use. Instead, I asked, "Where will we go?"

"Where's the last place they will look?" Erik shifted me in his arms but did not put me down.

"The middle of a city."

"They think we're unstable," Arne mused. "Without Fleur, we are. But she can tame the beast. With her, our control grows stronger every day."

Gunnr whined.

"We find a quiet place, on the edge of a busy village. Near enough to people that the Berserkers stay away," Arne continued. "We take a dwelling and blend in."

"Lords of this land willnae like it," Erik warned.

"We won't be there long enough to catch their attention. Just long enough to bond with our mate. Then we will return to the pack."

"We will?" I gasped. "But they'll kill you!"

"We hope not. By then we will have won the favor of our lady." Arne winked at me. Gunnr barked, tail sweeping back and forth.

"We cannae stay away from the pack forever, Fleur. Wolves are social creatures. We need the pack to survive."

"A lone wolf is a dead wolf."

"But...couldn't you make your own pack? The three of you?"

"Is that what you want? To be on the run with the three of us, and never see your sisters again?"

I didn't answer. My plan for them hadn't included me.

When Erik realized this, his expression darkened. "You willnae be rid of us so easily, Fleur. Last night was just the beginning. Soon we will finish what we started, and you willnae be able to deny the bond between us."

I remained quiet for the rest of the day's journey. Though I cared for them, I could not stay with these men. I still hadn't told them of my impending death. It seemed so cruel to snatch their hope away.

I could only hope when the Pack caught up, the Alphas would listen to me and be merciful.

"Something troubling ye, Fleur?"

We were traveling beside a rushing river. Every so often Erik would wade into the water and leap from rock to rock, marring our scent trail. Despite the high hot sun and his speed, he hadn't broken sweat. He held me high up on his chest, cradling me carefully even as he made his reckless jumps.

"Just worried about the pack catching up."

"Have faith in your mates."

He said it so sincerely, I couldn't roll my eyes.

When the river turned, we continued into the woods, where he set me down.

"Take a moment, lass. Stretch, do your business. But dinnae stray far."

I hurried behind a bush when I returned, Erik was frowning, rubbing his temples. His grimace fell away when I joined him.

I pretended I hadn't noticed and pointed to a patch of sky between the trees. "Is Arne flying as the eagle?"

"Aye. He says there'll be rain tonight. We'll find shelter for ye. Arne found a few places we could stay. Gunnr is running ahead in wolf form, scouting for us."

"So you often are on patrol like this?"

"Aye. Often enough. We are used to being away from the pack, though it wears on us after awhile."

We walked to the river to quench our thirst, and Erik offered me a bit of dried meat from his pack.

He kept rubbing his forehead while I finished the meat and washed my hands in the river.

"Are you all right?" I asked.

"Aye. 'Tis nothing. Come, we must be on our way."

While Erik carried me, I studied his face. Though he'd lived a century or more, he looked no older than a man of five and twenty. If not for his size and great strength, he would pass for a man I might have known from my old village.

"Careful," he growled, shaking me from my reverie. "We have another league to go, but I'll be setting ye down if ye don't stop staring."

"Sorry." I turned my head to watch the passing scenery, a blur from the speed he traveled. When we came to a worn path, grass growing between the wagon tracks, he slowed, but not by much. "I thought you said I could look at you."

"This has nothing to do with the pack rules, lass. I'm

happy for ye to look at me, especially if you're going to look at me like that. But I cannae stop to give into temptation."

"Oh." My cheeks flushed. Hot and aware of being in his arms. He carried me less like a sack of grain or an essential burden, and more like a man carries a woman over the threshold of the home he built for her. Perhaps it had always been so, and now I noticed.

Of its own volition, my finger traced the tattoo at the side of his neck. My soft body molded against his hard muscles. My nipples tightened to points.

He groaned, and changed directions, leaving the path and racing into the forest. When we reached a deep grove where the light barely broke the trees, he swung me down.

"Is everything all right?" I took a step or two back, trying to get myself under control.

A mistake, Erik's head swiveled to me, eyes gold, looking like the predator he was.

"Aye," he grunted, stalking forward.

"I'm sorry," I twisted my hands in my skirts. The fabric was a frail armor against the hunter's gaze. "I didn't mean to tempt your beast."

I made myself stand my ground. Erik closed the distance between us. His hands clamped on my hips and drew me against his body. My arms went around him automatically.

"'Tis no matter. Ye are always a temptation to me." I stilled as he bowed his head and buried his nose in my hair. "Ye smell so good."

"Shouldn't we continue on?" I whispered.

"My warrior brothers are meeting us here. Until then, I have a way to pass the time."

I gulped.

Slowly he set me away. "Soon we'll be at a private

dwelling Arne and Gunnr found for us, near a village full of people."

"That's good," I ventured.

"Before we go there, you must know the rules."

"Rules? For being with you?"

"Yes, and being our mate."

"All right." I would never be their mate. I needed to find a way to tell them.

Erik lifted the hair from my neck and laid his hand there, thumb and fingers almost collaring me.

"Rule one, we expect ye to give us perfect and complete obedience."

I wanted to jerk away, but his hand at my neck kept me still.

"We all answer to someone. Members of the pack fall into a hierarchy. The weaker submit to the stronger, and in turn the stronger protect them. Everyone, from the Alpha to a fragile and pregnant mate falls into this structure. Do ye ken?"

"Yes."

"Good. While you're with us, you'll submit to our rule and law. As a mate, you'll be expected to obey us always. We will fight and die for you. In return, you follow our lead so we can keep you safe. I know it can be hard," he lowered his voice to a sexy purr, "but do as we say and you will be sure to enjoy the reward."

I bit my lip to hold back my answer. It wouldn't hurt to go along with their rules. I'd already had a taste of them, living among the pack.

"What do you say, Fleur? Will ye obey our commands?" Erik asked, thumb stroking my pulse.

"Yes," I agreed.

"Good." He released me suddenly. "Let's have a test."

I raised my brows.

He jerked his head to the right. "Do you see that log?"

"Yes." The great tree had fallen some time ago, its branches held it a little way off the ground.

"Go there, lean over it and raise your dress."

My mouth dropped open.

"Do it."

To my annoyance, my feet started carrying me over there as soon as he gave the order. My body was primed and ready to please my handsome Berserker, even as my mouth asked in a petulant tone, "Why?"

He crossed his arms in front of him. "If you needed to know, I'd tell ye. Asking wastes precious time." His glare made my heart beat faster, and not with fear. What was happening to me?

Hands fisted at my sides, I paused halfway between him and the log. Finally I marched to the fallen tree and leaned on it.

"And your dress," he reminded me. The command weakened my knees and made my spine stiffen at the same time.

Cheeks burning and stomach tight, I lifted my skirts, baring my legs and my rump. The humiliating position made me grit my teeth, but I couldn't deny the trickle of excitement that made its way down my legs.

Erik was beside me in a flash, startling me, but I did not drop the dress.

"Good girl," he purred and a frisson of warmth curled through me at the endearment. His hard body crowded me, his hip leaning against the log as he passed a hand over my bottom. A shiver took me at the slight touch.

"Now you'll get your reward for obeying me. Soon, you will come to love it."

I didn't love being bent over and vulnerable to the large

warrior, but my back arched, pushing my bottom into his touch.

He chuckled. "Oh, yes, ye want this. Your mind hates submission but your body loves it. Place your hands on the log." I did and he held up my skirts with one hand, stroking my sensitive buttocks with the other. I dug my nails into the bark.

"I love ye like this. Bent over, helpless to my touch. I could order ye to assume this position twenty times a day and not have my fill." His hand strayed between my legs and I tensed, pushing myself up on tiptoe to escape his tickling touch.

"No, no," He laid a calming hand on my bottom. "Relax, wee flower. I'll touch ye when and how I wish."

I lowered back down.

"Good girl," he clucked again. "Now widen your stance and be still. I wish to see if ye are in heat."

I obeyed, draping my upper body onto the log, unable to hold myself up as he fondled me.

"So slick." His finger dipped between my folds. I squeezed my eyes shut to focus on the sensation.

"Do ye like that, Fleur?" One long finger dipped inside me and my knees inched together.

He slapped my right butt cheek and I yelped, rearing up.

"None of that." With the hand holding my skirts, he pressed me back down. His firm hand cupped my bottom and squeezed.

"What was that for?" I found my voice. The slap only stung a little, but was hard enough to leave a bright red print on my bottom, I was sure.

"Punishment," his voice held a grin. "Keep your legs open for your master."

Biting back a grumble, I lay back down on the log; his fingers delved again. My knees wobbled but didn't close.

He chuckled. "It seems that spanking is not quite a punishment for you."

"What do you mean?"

"Come here." He drew me up with an arm around my waist. Turning me, he had me clinging to him as his fingers brushed a pleasant spot and sent sparks dancing through me. I trembled and held my breath, waiting for more, but his hand drew away. "You're soaked. You may not like submitting to me, but your body craves it."

I jerked away. "I do not."

He smacked my buttocks three times in quick succession.

"Stop that," I hissed, and backed away, rubbing my tingling backside. The spanking hadn't quite hurt, but I still didn't like it.

Did I?

Erik guffawed and let me go.

"What's going on, brother?" Muscled arms wrapped around me, pulling me away from Erik. Arne's chuckle gusted my hair.

"Just a wee bit of punishment." Erik smirked. "Check her brother. I think she likes it."

"I do not," I protested louder.

Arne's fingers slipped between my legs, rubbing me, I squirmed away from the delicious feeling. "Even if you lie to us, Fleur, your body does not." He showed me his sticky digits.

I turned my head away, wrinkling my nose.

Arne released me, also laughing. He popped a finger in his mouth and sucked it clean, his eyes on mine.

"She is not in heat, not quite yet."

"We'll see what we can do about that." Arne's grin was wicked.

A short bark rang out.

"Gunnr is here to lead us to the home we found for us. Come, Fleur." Arne took my hand. My bottom and pussy throbbed as I trotted alongside him. I ignored it as best I could, but when Arne paused at a fork in the road to discuss the way with Erik, I drew up my skirt and checked my backside. The pale cheeks were unmarked.

"Disappointed, lass?"

I pulled down my dress, but not before Erik cupped my right bottom cheek in his hand and squeezed.

"Next time, wee flower, we will tie you down and spank ye until you're red. And if ye protest, we'll gag ye and pick a switch," his tone was mocking, but his expression was reverent as he fingered my smooth skin.

I pushed his hand away and wrenched down my dress. I had to get the situation—and my own responses—in hand. "You wouldn't dare."

"I would. I think you'd like it."

"I smell your cunny from here," Arne remarked. Both warriors loomed over me. Tall and broad, they could easily overpower me. My nipples hardened. I shivered, but they only took an elbow in each hand and escorted me to the place where we'd spend the night.

6

The hut stood on the edge of an empty field, boards blackened as if they'd been in a fire. My steps slowed, but the warriors moved me forward.

"Tis sturdier than it looks."

I made a face. "I'm not going to sleep in there. You need to find a cleaner place."

"Ye make many demands for someone who pledged obedience earlier."

"Perhaps we should pick a switch, just to be ready," Arne murmured.

"Come, lass. Trust your mates."

You are not my mates, I almost said aloud, but caught myself in time. Erik guessed my thoughts, judging by the determined look on his face.

As we approached, Gunnr the wolf stepped out of the door and woofed.

"Gunnr says it'll be better than sleeping under the rain. He spent all afternoon hunting for a nice, fat rabbit for your dinner."

When I hesitated to step inside, Erik swooped me up in

his arms and carried me over the threshold. Inside wasn't as bad as I imagined. The wall planks were sturdy enough, just dank and smelling of old smoke.

Erik set me down near the stone hearth. "There. Arne will get a fire going, and it'll be all the home ye could wish for."

With two men working at once, the fire was built up and the meat cooking. I helped by laying out the bedroll. With Erik's permission, I left with Gunnr to pick a few herbs that would make the meal taste good.

"It's not that I don't want you all as mates," I told him, walking with one hand buried in his dark fur. "I'm not like my sisters. I'm unfit to be anyone's mate."

The wolf whined unhappily.

Arne met me at the door when I returned. "Why don't you let us be the judge of whether you're fit or not."

Too late I remembered that warrior brothers could speak mind to mind. The entire pack could communicate this way, but these three's bond was closer, and anything I said to one, the rest would know.

"Come," Arne laid an arm around my shoulders. "Erik wants mead with our meal. We're to go into the village to see if they make a decent brew."

"Is it safe for us to go into the village?"

"Yes." He'd unfurled a rich looking cloak from one of the packs and wore it over his leather jerkin and breeches. He looked like a rich merchant, except when the robe blew back to reveal the axe and sword at his belt.

"What of the Berserker pack?"

"I laid a trail that will take them further north. It will buy us a little time. Long enough for you to get to know us."

"These villagers might not like strangers."

"There is a large market nearby and they are used to travelers. Stay close to me and do as I say."

We got some strange looks at the market, with just as many directed to Arne as to me. I supposed I did look as foreign as the Moor, with my flaxen hair tumbling over the fur cloak, the fine dress and thick fur lined boots. I looked like a warrior's bride, well-dressed yet wild. Plenty of men turned their head as I passed. Arne was all too willing to stare them down until their gaze snapped away.

With an expertise I wouldn't have guessed, Arne bargained for mead, dried fruit, and some grain. The vendors looked surprised by the amount of gold he carried, but they were nothing but respectful. As polite as he was, Arne was still a half a head taller than all of them.

Carrying our purchases, the handsome warrior strode along the vendors while I scuttled along beside. A flash of metal caught my eye, and distracted by a jeweler's stall, I nearly ran into a villager.

"Watch where you're going," the man spat.

A shadow fell over him, and he looked up, annoyance turning to horror. Arne's canines were out and they looked sharp. Looming over the villager, the Berserker snarled.

The man tripped over his feet to get away.

I sighed.

"What were you looking at?"

I pointed, and he guided me to the stall with a hand on my back. "Choose something," he nudged me.

I bit my lip, staring at the brooches. The vendor was a buxom woman with a sultry smile. Smiling and puffing out her chest to display her wares, she shared none of the fear most villagers had of the Berserker.

"Would you like to see this one?" She leaned over and

tucked her elbows in as she reached forward, deepening the cavern of her breasts.

"No," I said, a little too sharply. Arne frowned but waved in polite dismissal, and led me away.

"Was there nothing that you liked?"

"A little too gaudy for my tastes," I lied.

"And mine," Arne murmured.

I flushed.

"There is nothing in this market to hold my interest," the Berserker continued. "I already possess the loveliest thing here."

I shook my head.

He stepped in front of me and caught my chin, stilling the movement. "You disagree?"

My breath caught. I dared not speak, in case I burst into tears.

"You did not learn your lesson at the river," he chastised. "That's all right. We have many years to teach you."

"I don't..." my throat clogged for a moment. *I don't want to disappoint you. I am weak and unlovely, unfit to be a Berserker bride.*

His gaze gentled as if he heard my thoughts. "You are the mate we have chosen. We saw your courage from the first."

"I am...not strong."

"You are. You are powerful, Fleur. You are the only one who can break this curse on us, and set Gunnr free."

I started to open my mouth and he laid a finger over my lips.

"Do not fight it. I know you are afraid, but your mates are at your side, guiding you." He draped an arm around my shoulders, holding me in close confidence even as the market crowds swirled around us. "When I look at you, I see a bud tightly furled." He showed me his fist. "It is time to blossom, little one. It is time to become a flower." He opened his fist and presented me with a feather. After teasing my chin with it, he tucked it behind my ears.

"There," he murmured. "That is the only adornment you need."

He straightened, placing a hand on my back to guide me forward, and home. I took two steps and halted in my tracks.

A Grey Man blocked our path.

"Arne," I tugged his arm.

"I see him," the warrior's grim tone told me he knew the threat as well as I did. "There are some behind us as well. They appeared after I finished haggling for the mead."

"I've never seen more than one before." But sure enough, when I ducked my head to check, there were two of the lean creatures slinking after us.

"We're in a populated area. They may be doing work here for their master."

Arne hustled me away with an arm around my shoulders. We ducked around a stall and headed across a field for the woods. On the edge of the trees, Gunnr stepped out.

"I want you to go to him. On my word, you run and don't stop. Take a handful of his fur and follow his lead."

"What about you?"

"Never mind me." He drew his sword while his other hand steadied me. "Get ready. Run—"

I started picking up my skirts, a strange wind sent a prickle down my spine and I whirled.

"Arne!"

The Berserker stood to face the Grey Men, who kept slinking forward, eyes on me. Arne's left hand held the sword limp at his side. His right hand outstretched to stop them with some magic.

Gunnr ran forward, muzzle pulled back to show vicious teeth as he snarled at the Grey Men.

"We must go back and help Arne," I told him. "We cannot leave him."

The black wolf put himself between me and Arne and shoved me bodily towards the forest. I had no chance to resist.

A boom of magic and I fell onto my face.

Arms came around me and I cried out, but it was only Erik, lifting me.

"Arne. He's back there—"

"Quiet," Erik clipped. His frown looked more menacing with his beard.

I held my tongue until he set me down in the cabin.

"Where are your warrior brothers?"

"Safe. Which is more than ye would've been, if you'd stayed." Erik advanced, eyes burning. "What were ye thinking lass? Arne told you to run—ye must run."

I stood up. "I will not. I am sick of being treated like a weakling or a child. I can face the Grey Men. I've done it before."

"And been struck down with illness, again and again."

"I couldn't leave him."

"If ye were my mate," he bit off the words and strode to the fireplace, where he kicked a pile of wood with enough force to send it flying. Hand over his face, he leaned against the hearth.

My heart sank, but I didn't know why. He'd declared that I wasn't their mate yet. Wasn't that what I wanted?

Arne stormed in. "Fleur." Face blank but eyes tight with fury. "When I give an order, you obey. It's one thing to tease. Another to put your life in jeopardy."

"I didn't want to leave you." I crossed my arms in front of

my chest, steadying myself so I could stand up to the large warrior. "Whatever these Grey Men are, they are after me and only me. I don't want you risking your life for mine." Just because I could never have these men didn't mean I could bear to lose them.

"You didn't have a choice," he snarled. "You will never behave so recklessly again. I won't tolerate anyone putting you in harm's way—not even yourself."

"It's my life." I'd Seen my own death and accepted it. Seeing theirs would crush me. "I'll risk it as I choose."

"Not anymore. You belong to us."

"I will never belong to you."

Arne loomed over me, rage suffusing his face. I did not back down. I had to drive them away. I had to make them see: what we had was doomed.

Gunnr barked once and Arne stepped back at the sharp tone.

Erik turned from his place at the hearth. "We cannae do this. We don't have enough control."

"She must learn," Arne ground out. "We must train her to abide by the rules."

"Aye. But there are many ways to punish her."

"Tonight," Arne vowed.

❧

DUSK WAS ALREADY GATHERING when I went outside to let the warriors calm down. The weight of my men's disappointment a stone in my stomach, I sat on a stump with an arm laced around the wolf's neck.

"I know I did wrong, but I could not leave him. All these years, and I was the only one who saw the Grey Man, much less stood against him. I am used to absorbing their evil power and bearing the consequences. It may be all I am fit to do."

Gunnr licked my face. I wrapped my arms around him and buried my face in his pelt, surprisingly silky and soft. We waited like that while the line of trees swallowed the orange ball of fire.

My actions gnawed at me. These warriors had done nothing but risk themselves to protect and love me. They cared for me, and put my life above their own.

Perhaps they were worthy of my submission. Erik had spoken of obedience, and it rankled, but whenever I chose to bow to their rule, I felt peace. Was that another sign of my true nature? The spaewife magic that also caused my heated desires?

Gunnr whimpered and I loosened my grip on his fur.

"Whatever I do, defy or submit, it will be my choice. But I am tired of fighting my true nature. I have enemies enough." I bit my lip. Maybe I could follow the warrior's lead, for at least a little while.

"Fleur," Arne called from the hut entrance.

I rose to face whatever my warriors had planned. Submission wouldn't be easy, but if I trusted them to care for me, I could surrender. Deep down I knew they would never hurt me. The strict rules were part of how they cared for me. Besides, obedience soothed their beast. If it helped heal them, I could take a little punishment. I owed it to them.

Once inside, I took my place on a little stool they'd made for me from the section of a log.

Instead of standing over me, the warriors crouched close, all trace of anger washed away by worry.

Erik took my hand. "We need ye to understand something. Ye are everything to us."

I swallowed hard. Tears pricked my eyes.

"We have waited so long to have ye. We cannae lose ye. It would be our undoing."

Arne nodded in silent agreement.

"So we will guard ye carefully. Ye are never to go anywhere without one of us, ye ken?"

"I understand." I said in a hoarse voice. The hope and concern in their face made me want to weep.

"You belong to us, as surely as we belong to you. We knew it the moment we met you." Arne swept the robe around my shoulders, wrapping me in his scent.

"There is nothing we wouldn't do for ye. We will rid this island of Grey Men to make it safe for ye to walk anywhere you please."

"Until then, will you obey us? Help us protect you. We are not strong enough to lose you."

Gunnr pressed to my side.

"Yes. I understand. Forgive me."

"You're forgiven."

Arne stood, a lightness in their mien.

"Roast rabbit for dinner," Erik told me, gripping my knee before pushing up to go to the hearth.

"Wait," I also rose in confusion. "You're not going to punish me?"

Arne was in the corner, uncorking the mead. "There is a punishment we have thought of," he said, "but it may be too soon."

"I want it."

"Do ye?" Erik raised a brow.

I sighed. I had to be mad, but I'd vowed I would make it right. "I will accept whatever you give me. I'm strong enough."

"We know ye are. We wish to aid our bond with ye, not break it. Part of that is handling ye with care."

"I know you won't hurt me." My chin came up even though my stomach flipped like a fish out of water. "I'm yours to command."

The warriors exchanged a look.

"Very well," Arne came to a decision. "Off with your clothes."

I stripped quickly, trying not to think about it. After all, I'd been naked before at their command.

This time was different. When my dress and shift were piled on the bedroll, I shivered and not with cold.

"Good lass. So willing and obedient now. Why is that?"

"I want to please you."

Their smiles warmed me more than the fire.

"Come, lass," Erik held out his hand to invite me to sit on his lap again. "Even in battle, Arne remembered the mead."

We sat and ate as if it was an ordinary night. I was growing used to being naked around them, and having them enjoy my bare flesh more than the food.

As the mead flowed, the touching began, small strokes down my breasts.

Erik fed me a strip of luscious meat and left a finger in my mouth to suck clean.

At one point, Arne leaned over and casually cupped my bosom, thumb brushing against my nipple until it stood up tight and pink against my body.

He never stopped speaking about the market, the number of vendors, the quality of goods. The juxtaposition between their clothed bodies and my naked one made my heart pound. At any moment they might decide to take me, pull my body down to the bedroll and make me submit to delicious torment until I climaxed. Until then, I was a toy for them to play with, a pretty thing to pet and enjoy while they sat around the fire and drank.

Shifting, wet between my legs, I squirmed on Erik's lap, helpless against their casual, claiming touch.

By some unspoken signal, the men set their drinks down.

"It is time." Erik helped me stand on wobbly legs. Arne gathered me up and carried me to the bedroll where he laid me down. An eager expression on his face, he pinned me with his hard body and kissed me.

"The beast does not like it when you deny our claim over you, but that is all right. Your body tells us how you truly feel. We will train your body to accept us, and your mind will follow."

I didn't care what he did, as long as he kissed me again. His eyes crinkled in a knowing smile before he took my mouth again, his lips firm yet soft, demanding and claiming. When he was done kissing me, I gripped the edge of his jerkin, trying to get it off so I might press my skin against him.

"Not yet, little flower." He growled, and reached down and caught my wrist.

I pouted and he dropped his hips onto mine, rubbing against me. The hard length of his cock slid right over my ready channel. I whimpered.

He laughed. "There she is. Our little she-wolf, ready to go into heat for her mates." To my chagrin, he sat back. "Erik has something for you."

The black haired warrior leaned over and fed me strawberries by hand. Catching his hand, I sucked the juice from his fingers.

"So eager," he commented. "She will not long be able to deny her true nature."

"Let me," Arne said. He took a berry and rolled it over my lips. My tongue flicked out and he let some juice fall, staining them red. He smeared the berry juice down my chin and bare chest, drawing a line straight to my smooth cunny.

He came back up and kissed me, tasting the strawberry straight from my mouth, then kissed down my body, taking his time and suckling the places the berry had stained. As he went lower, he spread my legs.

"What are you doing?" I asked.

Firelight gleamed off the warrior's bald head.

"Tasting you." His teeth nipped my inner thighs and I jerked my legs together. His hands manacled my ankles and held them down. Erik held my wrists above my head.

Arne's head dipped again. His tongue swept up my lower lips, sucking as if he'd found the sweetest, ripest strawberry.

"Oh, goddess," I breathed.

"Like that?" Erik chuckled.

"More."

"Demands willnae get ye far, lass."

My hips rocked as Arne's tongue delved further, sweeping up and down my folds, flicking at the most pleasurable spots over and over. I shook in the warrior's iron grip. Somehow not being able to move made the sensation twenty times more intense.

As pleasure rose in me, my body tightened with need. Arne licked me to the brink, and just as I was about to go over, he stopped and sat up, wiping his mouth.

"What?" I raised my head off the blanket.

Erik let me go also. Both warriors were silent, studying me.

"Why did you stop?"

"This is your punishment. We deny you another night."

"No," I cried, and slapped the floor.

"Come, wee flower," Erik stripped off his jerkin and lay down beside me. "Time for bed."

My body ached, ending my plans to submit. Arne stretched out on the other side of me and I rolled to face him.

"I want you to finish."

He shrugged and closed his eyes, a smile hovering over his mouth.

"It's not right!" I cried. Desire clawed at me, turning me into a howling monster.

"It's not right that ye risked your life needlessly when your mates can protect ye."

"It's your choice, Fleur," Arne's deep voice rumbled at my back. "Either you belong to us or you don't."

I bit my lip until it almost bled, stopping myself from admitting what they wanted to hear. They could touch me and make my body respond, but I would not yield. It was for their own good.

Besides, I didn't need a man to pleasure me. Once Erik looked to be asleep, my own hand crept between my legs.

Without opening his eyes, the tattooed warrior caught it. "Oh no, lass. You will not touch yourself."

Everything about his body was relaxed but the grip on my wrist.

Arne pressed into my back. "You receive pleasure, or none, by our hands alone."

A growl escaped me.

"What's this?" Arne tugged my head back by my hair. "Does our she-wolf have a temper?"

"Ye will obey." Erik said.

"I hate you," I whispered.

Arne's large hand splayed over my midriff, pulling me closer.

"You will learn. This is your training."

"I-" I gritted my teeth before I could get the words out. If I gave them what they wanted, perhaps they would do the same. "I will not disobey again."

"We know."

Erik brought my hands to his lips and kissed them. "If ye do, we will have fun punishing you."

"Now, sleep, Fleur."

The warrior's breathing evened out, but Arne's thick member was still rock hard, pressing into my backside.

If I must suffer, so should they. I wriggled back into him.

The hand at my waist slid around me, his arm like an iron band keeping me still. "None of that now."

"Be good, Fleur, and, in the morning, we will reward ye."

With a sigh, I forced myself to relax. The throbbing between my legs was loud and insistent. Punishment indeed.

I was never going to be able to rest.

Arne's hold kept me from moving, but after awhile it loosened. The big warrior must be exhausted from his exertions against the Grey Men.

I felt a little guilty about that. It would be wise for me to get away from these Berserkers, and meet my fate alone.

On that unhappy thought, I closed my eyes and pretended to sleep.

~

THE FIRE FIZZLED AND CRACKLED, and I raised my head. On either side of me, my warriors were still asleep. Gunnr must be outside standing guard.

I stood up. My dress was gone, hidden somewhere, but I found my shift. I pulled it on. My cunny woke up and pulsed with readiness. Erik had promised satisfaction, but these men couldn't control me. I would slip away in the dead of night and find somewhere to tease my own flesh to completion.

Of course, when I returned in the morning, my punishment would be ten times worse, but that thought only made me more excited.

I reached the door before a voice stopped me.

"Where are ye going, Fleur?" Both warrior's eyes were open, gold in the dim hut.

"You will not like it if you make us chase you. We will catch you and there will be retribution."

A thrill went through me. "If you will not sate my body, I'll find someone who will," I hissed. Longing, mixed with fury, surged through me, giving my feet wings.

I ran into the night. The light rain was cool on my skin, but did nothing to dampen my ardor.

My whole body throbbed. I ran faster and faster down the path, driving forward into the mist until my shift was soaked. Panting and laughing, I spun in circles. I had to be mad. The Grey Men were out here; I should not be acting like this. But I was no longer the wasted, quiet, sickly Fleur. Inside of me was a wild and lusty creature, half goddess and half animal, all woman, and she was lulled by the call of the moon.

A cry broke out behind me. A howling wolf. I froze where I stood, entire body tense as I listened to the melancholy sound.

A second and third voice joined it.

My mates were singing to me.

Skin prickling with the eerie music, I trotted back. By the time I reached the open field, only one wolf was left singing. Gunnr.

He wasn't the one I was looking for. I veered away, and skidded to a stop. A growl sounded in front of me. I turned and ran the other way, skidding to a stop when another growl rang out almost at my feet.

Excitement tingled down my skin. This is what I wanted, what the feral part of me had been searching for. The chase. It was a game—I ran, and they came after me. My mates had to prove that they were strong enough to take me during a hunt. My blood hummed, body primed for the ancient rite.

I backed away slowly. Gunnr had disappeared, but two shadows closed in on me.

I whirled and ran.

It was over quickly. The shadow hit me and with an oomph I was lifted up, up, tossed over a warrior's shoulder.

I scratched his muscled back with my nails and he smacked my bottom.

"None of that." Arne.

Another shadow joined us. "Twas a short chase. What'll ye do now?"

"Tie her up in the rain," Arne grumbled.

"She'll catch cold."

Inside the hut, Arne swung me down. The two warriors crowded me.

"Obviously, the lesson didn't sink in," Arne frowned. "It's time we tried again."

"First, let's get her warm."

Arne stoked up the fire and heated some broth while Erik stripped me and chafed my flesh.

"If you're to be our mate, we need ye to obey."

I showed him my teeth. Whatever wildness had taken me, I was still in its grip.

"Her heat makes her as savage as our beast," Arne remarked.

"So wee and stubborn."

"Fortunately there are ways to make her behave." Across the hut, Arne lifted a rope.

"Dinnae worry, Fleur. Your mates will give you what ye need."

BY THE TIME the meat was cooked, I was stripped, tied and trussed in a humiliating display. Arne bound my arms first, binding my forearm to my upper arm.

"So you can't fight," he told me, and caught my left fist when I tried to punch him. He made short work my left arm, and had Gunnr hold me down with two paws on my back as he finished tying my legs. My calves to thighs, my limbs shortened.

"There she is, our sweet pet."

I bared my teeth at him.

"Time to eat." They placed a bowl in front of me. The meat swam in the broth, and saliva pooled in my mouth. The howling she-wolf inside me was hungry, but the rest of me hesitated.

All three of the warriors waited for me to bow my head and eat as if I really was their pet.

"You can't mean this."

"You wish to act like a wolf, we will indulge you. Nothing will stop us from caring for you as our own. You are hungry," Arne gestured to the bowl. "eat."

"I will not." My stomach gurgled in protest. "I cannot." I

dipped my head, testing how far down I could bend. I would have to lower my whole body just to get my face in the bowl.

"Poor lass." Erik took pity on me and lifted the bowl to my lips. I drank eagerly.

Arne stroked my haunch. "See how we see to your needs? In illness, in strength, when the wildness takes you, or when you are sweet. We can handle everything that you are. You will thrive within our care."

My meal ended quickly. Erik wiped my mouth. Arne's fingers kept swirling over my backside. I waited for them to dip into more secret places, but they never did.

Both warriors left for a moment, and the black wolf took their place.

Gunnr nudged me and I rolled to my side. He seemed to love my current state. I was on all fours just like him.

Arne set down meat for him to eat, and the wolf left, tail wagging.

I was on my back. When the warriors returned, my legs splayed open in blatant invitation.

"So ready for us." Arne seated himself next to me. They'd laid a blanket on the floor for me to pretend I was their pet; for that, at least I was grateful. "No more argument, then?"

Large hands teased my folds. My back arched, pushing into his touch.

"So naughty. Next time you run, we tie you up like this and strike your pussy until you come."

He laughed at my shocked expression. "You do not think it is possible? I'll tell you now, there are more delights your body can give us than you can ever imagine."

"Speaking of which, brother," Erik said. "Time to start training her wee arse."

They set me on all fours again. I craned my neck to see what they would do.

After smearing oil between my bottom cheeks, Erik probed my back hole.

I yelped and jerked forward.

"Oh no, ye don't."

Arne caught me and held me still, while Erik smacked my bottom until it wobbled.

"Be still. We'll soon reward you." Arne's fingers closed on my nape, that comforting, dominating gesture that made me clay in his hands.

I rested in the bronze warrior's arms while Erik played with my arse, tickling the rim of my dirtiest hole, pushing in until I gritted my teeth.

His other hand came to play with my pussy and my whimper turned into a moan.

"That's it. Relax and let us train your bottom for us. One day you will accept our cocks into your body. We will claim you together."

I shivered at Arne's dark promise.

Erik's oiled finger slid into my pussy just as another penetrated my tight bottom hole. He held me this way, pinching my aroused flesh until my inner walls rubbed together. I panted, overcome with deep pleasure. My bound limbs trembled.

My orgasm crashed over me. Both my holes spasmed, opening like mouths in a silent wail.

"There's a good lass," Erik said. He washed his hands as Arne untied me and rubbed circulation into my flesh.

Once out of bondage, my voice returned. "Will you fuck me?"

"Soon." He kissed me. "Very soon."

An ache spiraled through me, but it was a happy one. I

was content to wait. These men proved again and again that they would give me what I needed.

"So sweet and submissive," Arne stroked my hair. "You delight and entice us, no matter what mood you're in."

"'Tis late," Erik said with a yawn. "Even later than the first time we laid down to sleep. Time for bed, wee wolf."

"First, there is something we have for you." Arne went to rummage in the pack, and returned with a slim silver torc, a little larger than the arm ring many of the Berserkers wore to declare their allegiance to the pack. Bending it, he widened the opening.

"Kneel, Fleur, and lift your hair."

After a moment's hesitation, I did so. He slipped the silver ring around my neck and closed the gap. His finger ran around it, checking the fit.

He helped me to my feet, looking very pleased.

"This marks you as ours."

"Be warned, Fleur, you will wear more than just the torc as proof you belong to us."

The warriors pulled me to the bedroll, and once again took their places at my side.

I looked for Gunnr before laying my head down, but the midnight wolf was gone.

I DREAMT OF A MAN, tall with black hair and golden eyes. He ran from me, keeping just inside the edge of shadows where I dared not tread. Finally I called his name, "Gunnr!" but he gave me a sad look, and turned and disappeared.

When I woke I stared at the ceiling of the hut for as long as the warriors let me lie. Last night had been the turning point. I had submitted. I now wore their torc. The beast within me, whatever she was, wanted nothing more than to entice, and be dominated by her mates.

The more level headed Fleur knew this brief holiday would end all too soon.

Eventually, the pack would catch up, and the warriors would die. Or the Grey Men would close ranks and we all would.

"So serious, lass." Erik leaned over me. "Dinnae start your morning with a frown. Arne and Gunnr will return soon. In the meantime, I have a wee gift for ye."

He showed me a carved piece of wood much like the dowel they'd used to take my virginity, only this was a bulb shape with a narrow stem topped with a flat circle.

"What's that for?"

"You'll see, soon enough. Come on now, lass. Head down, arse up, and part your bottom for me."

"What?" I blanched.

"Didn't you promise to obey?"

I moved into place with a sigh. Cheek to the bedroll, I reached back, but just couldn't bring myself to complete the action.

"Still shy around your mates? Perhaps ye need some motivation." Two fingers slid along my lower lips. "Do as I say and there's more like that for ye."

My cunny had already started to drip. Resigned, I took a fleshy globe in each hand and showed Erik my bottom hole.

"Good lass."

He cleaned me carefully, a wet cloth probing my most intimate areas, followed by a little oil.

"Now," he said. "I'm going to put this plug in your ass and make ye come for me."

"No..." I dropped my arms, but he'd already set an oiled finger at my pucker. It tickled and burned, stretching the intimate place. He played with me for what seemed like hours. My body grew slick and excited from his taboo attention. Arousal and humiliation both pooled deep in my belly.

Finally his fingers had stretched me enough to set the bulb into place.

"Good lass. Ye can sit up."

I rose, face flushed. My hand went to the wooden piece in my ass and he tutted. "None of that. Keep it in like a good girl and there'll be a reward."

My ass felt full, like there was a giant wedge splitting me. It would be impossible for me to walk, sit or even stand still without noticing its presence.

"Once your body gets used to that, we can get ye one larger," Erik commented.

My eyebrows shot up but I made no comment until he'd gone to the fire to dish up some breakfast.

"I hate this," I muttered.

Too late I remembered that wolves have excellent hearing.

"Oh?" Erik returned with the food bowl, and instead of handing it to me, he sat and tugged my hand so I sat in his lap, bottom balanced so my position didn't drive the plug further into me. "Your body says otherwise. Even now it is wet and ready."

I squirmed.

"One day the three of us will take ye together in each hole. Here," He touched my mouth, "Here." He handed me the bowl and cupped my slick cunny. "And here." His fingers dipped back to tap the plug. "Even now, it's all we can do to keep from throwing ye down and fucking ye hard."

One arm crooked around me to steady me, but the other cupped my hot and wet center as I ate.

"Why do you wait?" I asked around a mouthful.

"We want to be ready. Soon, Gunnr will be a man, and the three of us can claim ye together."

I blinked, remembering my dream.

"He is afraid to Change. What if the beast overtakes him?"

Erik sighed. "We are doing all we can to keep that from happening."

I chewed slowly. Erik didn't ask me how I knew of Gunnr's struggle. My dream must be part of the growing bond.

"There's that frown again. What are your thoughts, Fleur?"

"I'm not sure if I can help you as much as you think," I said.

"Let us be the judge of that. We believe the magic between us is working. So far you've responded to everything we've done."

I scowled.

"Ye say you don't like it, but ye do. Ye liked it last night even when we bound ye and made ye our wee pet."

"That was not me. The heat disturbs my mind, makes me...into something I am not. Your beast infects me."

"The beast is part of us, Fleur. Our savage desires are as much a part of us as our kindness or logic. But together, we will help each other stay in balance. Perhaps it takes a true mate to see our darkness and accept it. Once someone loves the whole of us, we can be who we truly are."

I'd finished eating while he was talking. Again I waited until he was across the hut, putting out the fire before I whispered the truth.

"I still do not like that part of me."

"That is why ye can't accept us as mates. Ye have to accept yourself, first." Erik rose, rubbing his hands together.

"Fortunately ye have three Berserkers to tell ye how perfect ye are."

After braiding back my hair, he produced my dress and helped me into it, and knelt to help me lace up my boots. The finishing touch was the fur cloak.

Erik stepped back to take me in. "Ye still don't think you beautiful?"

I shrugged.

"Come, then."

Outside, under a clear sky, he led me to a small pond in an empty field. "Look there."

I bent over the water, expecting to see a blurred shape backed by clouds. Instead, my face stared back, pure and in color. My cheeks were pink and healthy under my fair hair. With the fur cloak and fine dress, I looked like a barbarian queen. Lovely and wild, but not weak or frail at all.

"What magic is this?"

"My magic," a woman's voice rang out.

7

A blonde woman, her hair braided into a crown came forward, walking with a staff and a raven flying over her.

Erik stepped between her and me.

"Yseult," he greeted her. I peered around him, wanting to see the witch who had told the pack where to find my sisters and I, so the Alphas could make us brides. The witch was tall and beautiful, with a cold, impersonal mien. The raven landed on top of her staff and cocked his head at me. There was more expression in the beaked face than in Yseult's, as if she could only mimic human expression because she had no natural feelings of her own.

"So this is Fleur. The strongest sister. I have long been kept from meeting her."

I spoke before I could stop myself. "Strongest?"

"You are youngest so you think you are least?"

"Fleur," Erik cautioned.

"No, it is because I have often been sick."

She nodded. "Magic always has a price. The greater the power, the greater the price." Her head snapped to

Erik, a bird-like movement. "So, you wish me to train her?"

"We wish to bargain with you for some answers," Erik spoke slowly and carefully. "As long as the price is reasonable."

"And if my price is her?" Yseult tilted her head to indicate me.

High in the sky, an eagle screamed.

Erik growled, "You cannae have her."

"No? But you are so weak, wolf. You've come so far, and fought so hard, and the hardest part of the journey is yet to come." She raised a hand and swept it through the air in front of her. The raven launched itself into the air and flew in lazy loops above our heads.

Erik closed his eyes, beads of sweat appearing on his forehead.

"Even now you resist the call of the pack, your Alpha's anger," Yseult continued in a low, soothing voice. "It takes its toll. Who will save your lady love, when the beast consumes you?" Spoken in that lulling, seductive tone, her words wormed their way inside my head. My body felt weighted by them. I fought to take a step forward, even as Erik swayed beside me.

"Stop it," I whispered. I grabbed Erik's hand and he gripped it tightly, so hard it brought tears to my eyes. Pain refreshed my mind and I found the strength to screech, "Stop it!"

Yseult's half lidded eyes flew open. The golden eagle dropped from the sky, hurtling straight towards the slowly circling raven. The black bird disappeared into the brush with an ungainly squawk.

The eagle stopped short before hitting the ground. It's great wings swooped up and became a man's muscled arms.

Arne stood there, fully clothed in a sleeveless jerkin, leather breeches, and a richly woven cloak flowing down behind him.

I'd never seen a Berserker complete the Change wearing more than a loincloth. The very air shivered with the completion of such showy magic.

"Witch," Arne rumbled, striding towards her. "We are not so weakened that we cannot protect our mate from you." He stopped a few feet away, and though I knew he was much, much bigger than the blonde woman, somehow she seemed just as tall.

"So you have claimed her then." Yseult pointed her staff at me. Both warriors snarled as if she'd drawn a weapon. With a smirk, she tipped the staff back up and away from me. "Congratulations. I see she wears your torc willingly."

I touched the silver piece around my neck.

"Have you completed the mating process?"

"That is not your concern."

"Still unmated then." She chuckled, then jumped as the midnight wolf pushed through the grasses at her back. Gunnr trotted over to us, baring his teeth at the woman as he went.

"And now I see why you cannot yet mate," she murmured. Tense seconds passed. My skin prickled with the weighted silence. My sisters had told me the witch was dangerous, but in the past had come to their aid.

With a funny little sound that might have been a laugh, but came out wrong and grating, the witch broke the quiet. "I've decided to help you. Please, sit down." Yseult swept out her hand again, and there were three stones in a row, perfect for us to sit. Erik took one, but kept me on his lap. Arne stood beside us while Gunnr sat on his haunches. I reached up and took Arne's hand, and put my other on Gunnr's back.

Yseult fussed with her skirts. By the slight curve of her mouth, she seemed pleased.

"Now, why did you summon me?"

"We have a problem," Arne said. "There is an evil I've detected. It is trapped in one area, from what I can tell, but it has many mobile servants. And they are drawn to Fleur."

"They seek all spaewives," Yseult said.

That did not reassure me at all. Erik and Gunnr both growled.

"Why?" Arne asked. "And why did you not tell us this sooner?"

"I told the pack where to find Fleur and her sisters, did I not?" She shrugged and was met with stony silence. Sighing, she continued. "Do you ever wonder why Berserkers exist?"

The three warriors stiffened.

"We came to be because the witch cursed our human selves," Arne spoke slowly, as if educating a child.

"Yes, but how did that witch know that curse?"

"She was evil. She wrought it from her sorcery."

"Yes she was evil, but she did not have the power to create the curse. Only to repeat it. And try as she might, she was no sorceress."

"Explain."

Yseult settled in to tell the story, long fingers stroking the runes of her staff. "Long ago a king wished to have great power. He was already very, very dangerous, but the power he dealt with had long ago eaten his mind and he was willing to do anything for more.

As I've said, every bit of magic requires sacrifice. Witches and warlocks sacrifice small things— a rabbit here, a dove there. Larger spells require a bigger animal such as a goat."

"The witch who cursed us sacrificed a pack of wolves," Erik said, his voice a bleak reflection of the horror of that night.

Yseult nodded. "The larger the sacrifice, the greater—and more evil—the power. This king knew that, and sacrificed great things. He was beyond the level of warlock or mage. He was a sorcerer."

"So, what did he sacrifice? Humans?"

"Yes." Her voice dropped. "He killed his own children to feed his necromancy."

I let out a whimper, and Erik pulled me closer.

"The king kept many wives. He found the women blessed with natural magic--the spaewives. Their progeny had elements of both their blessed mother and their evil father. When the king killed them and consumed their flesh, he grew more powerful still. He was close to being strong enough to bring the whole world to heel, when one of his wives realized his awful plan.

She called upon the full moon, the goddess, who gave her a spell. The woman cast the spell over her children, all sons. They became wolves, and more than wolves; Berserkers. They were strong enough to overpower their father, and his forces. They struck him down, and with their mother's help, bound him with magic and threw him into the sea.

But he did not die. His cold remains came to this island, and floated up the river, until it rested in a tomb of its own making. Over the centuries he has grown stronger. He attracts men to his grave, consumes their mind with his magic, and makes them serve him."

"The Grey Men," Arne said.

"Yes. So now he sends his servants out to gain the power to rise again. And once he has he will not stop until he has enslaved every spaewife to his lust, and forced them to bear his children. The cycle will start all over again, unless you can stop it." And she looked straight at me.

Eriks' arms tightened around me. "Fleur? What can she do?"

"Never." Arne gripped my hand. "We will never let her near them. We will take her and run."

"There is nowhere on earth you can go. Even now he is strong, too strong. If I had been more powerful, years ago, I would've faced him, but by the time I could, he was more powerful still."

"We will not risk our mate. Never."

"The Grey Men will not stop coming," the witch warned.

"Then we will kill them. All of them." Arne dropped my hand and advanced. His fingers were tipped with vicious claws.

Erik also rose and set me behind them.

"Stop," I said. "You grow too angry. Yseult is not the enemy." I pulled both men back, as I did, I mouthed to Yseult. "I will speak to you alone."

Very well. Yseult's voice echoed in my mind. I sucked in a breath, but smoothed my expression when the warriors whirled on me.

"We leave, now," Erik ordered. They took hold of either arm, and followed the midnight wolf, striding away.

IT WASN'T until late that night, when I rose to relieve myself, that I passed a puddle of rainwater and met Yseult's reflection.

"We do not have much time," she said. "Even now, the pack is closing in on one side, the Grey Men on the other."

"Tell me, then." I said. "How do I stop the Grey Men, and the rising?"

"Bond with your warriors. Bring them back to the pack with this news. United they will stand against anything."

I touched the silver ring around my neck. Earlier, they'd taken the plug out, told me I'd wear the torc for the rest of my life. "We have been trying to bond—"

"Try harder. Do not fight it. You can bond with them, if you allow it."

I shook my head. The witch seemed so sure that once my mates and I bonded, we could avert all disaster. It made me wonder what she knew. "Yseult, why do you help us? When you first met with Erik and I, you tried to cast a spell."

"You broke it easily enough, Fleur." One shoulder came up in a half shrug. "It is my nature to test. I need the Berserkers at their fighting strength. Weakness cannot be tolerated. That is why I found you and your sisters for them. I cannot face the Corpse King alone."

"Why are you involved in this fight?"

"Because I was once like you. The Grey Men came for me but I had no protector. I performed every sacrifice I could, seeking power to fight him, and crossed the line into darkness. I have power, yes, but it is unnatural and burned my goddess-given magic out. I am no longer a spaewife, nor able to be a mate to a Berserker." There was regret in her voice, the most human she'd ever sounded. "But I am safe for a time. If the Corpse King rises, that all ends. There is no magical creature he does not desire to rule over, or destroy." Was that a touch of human fear in the flat tone? "I dare not get close to his resting place. Even now I search for the spell to destroy him, because once he wakes, there is no way to lay him to rest."

"One of his wives found a way," I reminded Yseult.

"Yes, and that spell has been lost."

I knotted my hands together. So much depended on me laying aside my fears, and opening myself to my men. "The goddess will reward you for helping us," I said finally.

"I will not lie to you, Fleur. If you do not bond to your warriors in time, you may face the Corpse King without them. I have not seen the outcome of that. There are several paths the world can take, but the fate of this island rests on you."

My fingers rose again and stroked the torc around my neck.

"I can give you a few tricks that may help." Yseult's voice grew more faint and further away, and the puddle rippled, marring her image.

"Fleur?" one of the warriors called from inside the hut.

"Coming." As I rose, my foot dashed the water and Yseult's face swirled away.

Meditating on the witch's words, I nearly tripped over something lying on the hearth.

The witch's staff.

8

"I don't like it," Erik growled. He stood with arms folded, scowling at the long carved piece of wood Yseult had left. Probably one of the "tricks" she'd left to help me, though I hadn't offered that as an explanation as to why it appeared outside our hut in the middle of the night.

"The witch never does something without reason," Arne said. He looked tired, more tired than he should've looked for simply being woken in the middle of the night. Being away from the pack was beginning to wear on all of them. "This may protect Fleur, or may not. But it is a gift, and not easily spurned."

"She wants Fleur to face these things, to fight this ancient evil. I will die before I allow that to happen."

Gunnr whined.

"Stop fighting." I said. "It's upsetting our bond."

Erik turned away, but not before I saw him wiping some blood away from his face. Another nosebleed from mental strain.

"Whatever it is—an aid or a trick—we can do nothing

about it until morning." Arne already was lying back on the bedroll. With a few more grumbled comments, Erik rejoined us. I didn't tell him that I felt safer with the staff present, even with it on the far side of the room where Erik had kicked it after I brought it in.

The witch was right: time was running out, and we needed all the aid we could get.

I DREAMT AGAIN of Gunnr in man form.

He was a tall and broad-shouldered man, naked but for the black pelt around his shoulders. There was a little white scar under his eye, just where the few white hairs were on the wolf.

"Fleur," he grunted, a guttural sound I could barely understand. I was bound somehow, and he knelt over me, slicing through the bonds so I could hold him.

My fingers sifted through his silky dark hair. I pressed my lips to his smooth skin. My legs locked around him, pulling him into my body, and he drove into me with a cry. I smiled as I absorbed his thrusts into my body.

When he shuddered in orgasm over me, I tightened my hold.

His lips found my ear. "So sweet and perfect." He sounded less like an animal, more like a man.

I smoothed back raven dark hair from his face. He was golden-eyed and tan as a dried oak leaf, a shade between Arne and Erik's. "Do you have to go back?"

"I dare not stay."

Craning my neck, I kissed him. *I will bring you back forever,* I promised, speaking mind to mind. *I will find a way.*

THE NEXT MORNING, the strange chill in the air matched the frosty silence between Erik and Arne. I huffed and, taking up the staff, went to get water with Gunnr.

We walked in silence. My heart was too heavy to speak of what I had seen in my sleep. From the wolf's sad mien, I wondered if we'd shared the same dream.

A snarl rang out from the woods as we neared the stream. Gunnr immediately pushed in front of me, forcing me back. I didn't need a second warning to run. We raced back, Gunnr at my heels, with the growling sound behind us. As I neared the hut, I placed the sound. Not wolf. Berserker.

"Come, Fleur," Arne burst out of the hut. He grabbed my hand and pulled me along. Just his touch made me faster than I would've been otherwise. The staff also gave me a weightless feeling that made me light on my feet.

Erik and Gunnr, both in wolf form, disappeared into the woods.

Arne kept us running forward. "They'll create a confusion in the trail while we hide in the village."

"What about the Grey Men? Won't they be waiting?"

"We must try."

We broke out of the woods, into the field where the witch had laid the scrying glass. Grasses whipped my skirts, but the land gave way to a boot-sucking mud.

"Moons," Arne cursed. The pond in the field had turned into a giant pool of water. I made the mistake of looking down, and instead of my face and figure, I saw my death vision—the cloth wrapped corpse in the tomb-like cave.

"Fleur," I came back to Arne shouting in my face.

"What was it?"

"I saw my grave," I told him, clutching his arms. We both knelt on the edge of the water.

The baying of the hunting pack grew louder.

"Hold on," he said, shifting his body so he was between me and the shaking grasses.

A figure burst from them, a giant black furred monster. I clutched at the staff as if it was a weapon, but it had no tricks to help me.

"Erik," Arne spread his hands to show he was no threat. "'Tis us."

The canines and fur receded until I recognized some of Erik's face. The creature's body was hunched, grown a foot over his already massive size. Gunnr at his side.

"Is the pack gone?" I asked in vain hope.

"No," Arne said. "We're surrounded." The warriors formed a circle with me at the center.

"Are the Alphas here?"

"All of them. I am sure of it."

"We can escape right?" I asked even as my heart sank. Arne could turn into an eagle, but what of the others? They could not just fly away.

Erik dropped to one knee beside me. His hands were more like claws tipped with razors, but his face was now mostly man.

"Fleur, go. They will not hurt ye."

"No," I clutched his arm. "Not without you."

"We've been here before," Arne rumbled. "There is no time."

"I tell ye to run, ye run."

"I cannot. I won't let you die."

"There is a chance that, if we give you back, the Alphas will let us go."

"You will be cut off from the pack. I heard your thoughts. You will go mad and die."

"There is not much time." Arne ground out. "And there is no leniency in them."

"They come to kill us, Fleur, we do not wish you to see it.
"

"No, I won't allow it. I shouted. I swung my staff out, and struck the ground. It splashed in the water, which was now rising enough to cover our feet. The scrying pool kept spreading, stretching out from us in all directions.

Arne stumbled in surprise. "What magic is this?"

"No time," I cried. "Hang onto me." My left hand dug into Gunnrs' fur, and my right hand drove the staff into the water again. Mist was pouring from the surface of the water, spreading over the fields.

"Keep your hands on me," I ordered and waited until Arne and Erik grabbed either arm. "Now we walk. Slowly."

Our movements didn't disturb the mist, which kept pouring from the surface of the water, thicker wherever the staff touched.

Through it we saw shadowy shapes, the hulking monsters of Berserkers in the grip of rage. Sometimes the snarls and howls of Berserkers sounded closer, sometimes far away.

"Some of our brothers may fall in this," Arne muttered.

"It will not hurt them."

"No, but panic might leave them little more than raving beasts."

I struck out for the far side of the magical pool, but to my surprise, the hut appeared in front of us.

"This place is safe, Arne said. "It is warded. I feel the Berserkers will not find us here, otherwise it would not appear."

The warriors made me enter first. Out of respect for Erik, I left the staff leaning on the wall by the door, though he didn't seem to mind the witch's tool any longer.

I took the few steps it took to reach the pallet and sagged down immediately. Exhaustion pooled in my body, weighting my limbs.

Arne knelt by the bed to cover me with the fur cloak. I caught his hand. "Being separated from the pack takes its toll. We need to bond."

"Rest, little one," he soothed in his deep voice. "There will be time for that, goddess willing."

I woke to the smell of wet fur, and a heavy warmth at my back. Without opening my eyes, I twitched, and started to roll away, when a rough tongue caught my cheek.

Gunnr's long nose poked me as he licked my face.

I wrinkled my nose. He grinned at me, and let out a bark. Arne hastened to my side.

"How are you feeling?" he asked, and helped me sit.

I did an inventory of my limbs. My body was stiff but nothing hurt.

When I told Arne this, he blew out a relieved breath and gave me a cup of mead.

"You saved us, Fleur."

I offered a weak smile. "Perhaps the staff is useful, after all."

"Or you've finally come into your strength," Erik crouched close.

"Are we still safe here?"

"Night has fallen. If there are Berserkers out there, we cannot sense them. We believe the mist led them astray."

"We have a reprieve."

I set the cup of mead down. "We must bond." I said.

"Oh yes, little mage? Do you order us once again?" Arne said in an amused tone as he rose and went to the hearth.

"Will ye threaten us with your staff if we do not comply?"

"Do you threaten me with yours?" I gave the front of his breeches a pointed look.

Erik guffawed. "I think that punishment is in order."

"Oh yes," Arne said, returning with the pack of things he purchased at the market. "You disobeyed us yet again. We told you to run, and you refused."

"It saved your life," I pointed out what he himself had told me just a minute ago.

"Yes," he grinned as if he knew his own illogic. "But when we give an order we expect you to obey. We will train you until you do."

Tingles spread through my body.

Erik tugged a lock of my hair. "The beast requires restitution. It wants you to submit, to know you belong to us."

Smiling, I pulled the thong out of my hair and let it tumble down my shoulders. "Do what you will."

A FEW MINUTES LATER, I lay naked on my back, tied spread eagle in the center of the hut. The ropes were made of soft leather, and tied around four large rocks.

Our enemies might be without, but I had no cares in the world.

"Deep breath, lass," Erik ordered.

I obeyed, letting him rule my very breath. Bound as I was, I could only move my head or twitch a finger.

Arne sat on a rock above me, holding a lit candle—another recent purchase from the market.

Erik lay on his side next to me, lazily cupping one of my breasts.

"And now, Fleur? Do you agree to obey us? Do as we command?"

I turned my head towards him. "Only if it doesn't put your life in harm's way."

"Wrong answer," Arne tipped the candle and white wax spilled from the top, falling on my exposed flesh. I flinched as each drop touched my skin, little points of fire that lined my collarbone like a necklace.

I lay on the soft cloak of pelts, but not a drop of wax touched the fur.

"Who do ye belong to?" Erik asked. His fingers strayed lower, gliding over my vulnerable belly and dipping inside my cunny.

"I belong to you."

"Are you sure?"

His fingers slid lower and I clenched my bottom as much as I was able against his assault.

He tsked me. "A little encouragement," he said to Arne, who let the wax spatter my breasts. My back arched and I gasped.

Settling between my legs, Erik slicked his fingers and drove a finger and thumb into either of my nether holes.

"How about now?"

Leaning closer, Arne dripped wax right on my nipple, making my body clench hard around Erik's invading digits.

Arousal blazed through me.

Erik delved deep in my folds, thumbing a sensitive spot that drove the blaze higher. More wax splashed over my left nipple and the fire inside threatened to consume me.

"Tell us what we want to hear, Fleur, or we'll coat your body with every bit of wax and still won't let you climax."

"Oh, please." Every muscle in my body tightened, fighting for the pleasure just out of reach.

"Let me plug her," Erik said. "She'll remember who owns her body when she has a full arse."

My warriors pushed the stones at my left and right feet closer so they could prop my bottom up. Erik produced the wooden bulb and oiled it to a polish.

"No," I moaned as he pressed it between my bottom cheeks.

"Ye say no, but your nipples are pointed and your cunny leaks with desire." Erik swirled the narrow end of the plug around my bottom hole, tickling the sensitive flesh. "I think ye like it."

"She likes knowing she's owned. That every part of her is ours to command. And we will punish or pleasure her as we wish."

Stretched out on the pelts, with firelight glimmering on my wax-spattered skin, I was their beautiful possession.

My head lolled on my neck as the plug stretched my bottom hole to its max, and slid right in.

Arne kept dotting my skin, dropping the wax from different heights as if testing my reactions as Erik fucked me slowly with the plug. Sweat beaded on my skin along with the wax.

"Please." My limbs trembled with the advent of pleasure.

Erik stretched me with two fingers in my cunny, then another, and another. "Soon we will fill you."

"Tonight," I gasped. "Please."

"You do not set the rules," Arne reminded me. "You submit to our rule."

I bared my teeth at him, and he laid a trail of wax

droplets from sternum to my shaved mons. My midriff clenched with each addition, the heat building and building as Arne's design came closer to where Erik played.

With a wicked grin, Erik pulled out his fingers, and then the plug, just as Arne dripped the wax right on my hot center.

My cries rang in my ears as my climax shattered my very mind.

The warriors stood over me, breeches open and cocks out. Erik had his in hand and grunted as he worked it. Arne's powerful thighs quivered as he fisted his giant rod.

I jerked in my bonds, licking my lips.

"Please. Give me your cocks. Grant me what I need." Under the hardened wax, my nipples throbbed.

"You take what we give you," Arne said. His jaw clenched. He knelt and I strained upwards, scenting his musk. Fluid leaked from the tip of the flared head.

Erik knelt on the other side of me. One hand kept pulling on his cock as the other closed over my breast.

My lips mouthed "please, please," as the warriors splashed me with their seed.

They broke my bonds with their bare hands and lifted me, each claiming my mouth before washing me with soft clothes and wrapping me in the fur cloak.

Arne gathered me into his arms. "We will not take you until all of us can take you together."

"There is no time. The Grey Men come. The Corpse King wants me for his bride."

Arne pressed a soft kiss to my temple. "He will not take you. You already belong to us."

～

ARNE STOOD in the doorway of the hut, bathed in morning light. I rose and pulled the cloak around me more tightly as I went to him. He put his arm around me but did not speak. The mist still curled through the forest and field, but was dying away.

"There are no signs of the Berserkers, though we know they still hunt for us. Erik and Gunnr scouted as wolves."

I shivered in the cool air. It did not feel like midsummer any more.

"Come back inside."

He banked up the fire as I stood by with my arms wrapped around my body.

"Arne, the claiming...it is not complete, is it?"

"Not yet. Gunnr dares not Change."

I rubbed my face, feeling all the weariness of the past few days.

And it was not only me. The warriors were showing signs of strain. Erik rubbing his pained head and getting nosebleeds. Gunnr stuck as a wolf. Even Arne's broad shoulders were beginning to stoop, his beautiful skin turning sallow. It was more than just separation from the pack. My sickness infected them.

The door creaked as Erik and Gunnr returned, but I couldn't face them.

"It's my fault," I whispered.

"No," Arne said, reminding me that werewolves have sharp hearing. "We need more time."

"We run. Stay away from both the pack and the Grey Men."

I picked up Yseult's staff. "I can go back. I will plead your case."

"You will not," Erik said.

"You don't understand. I cannot bond with you."

"Of course you can," Arne said. "You have the magic and you care for us—"

"I am dying." My cry filled the hut. "I know I am. I saw my own death." Three stricken faces fenced me in, two warriors, one wolf. "I saw a tomb in a cave, and a body wrapped in cloth."

"Fleur." Arne stepped forward.

"No." I threw up a hand to ward him off, but too late. Erik's tattooed arms closed around me and the staff fell with a clatter.

"Hush, hush." He pawed at my hair, squeezing me close as if reassuring himself that I lived. "We will not let anything happen to ye."

There was nothing they could do.

"Do not say that," Arne said.

I blinked. I hadn't spoken aloud, which meant the warriors had heard my thoughts.

Yes, Erik spoke into my mind. There is a bond between us. Ye cannae deny it.

"It's too late. It's not safe for you to be connected to me. You cannot risk it."

"We'll be the judge of what we will or will not risk."

"I-" Before I could finish my thought, Erik whipped me around to face him,

Fisting the hair at the back of my head, he bowed my body backwards and kissed me. His lips were hard, desperate, and I refused to yield before him. I fought, hands tugging at his bare shoulders, nails scratching his powerful muscles until he shuddered but did not let go. His tongue thrust into my mouth.

My body caught fire. I pressed against him, rubbing my aching nipples. Instead of pushing him away, I clawed at his back, trying to get him closer.

His hands found my bottom and cupped it, lifting me. My legs twined around his hips as he carried me to our sleeping place, and laid us both down. His lips released mine and returned, beard scratching my face. Back arching, I took his head in my hands and forced him down, so his stubble would scrape my needy breasts.

"By the moon," Erik breathed. His hands tore open the cloak I wore, and I was grateful my shift and dress were safely folded away. They would not survive the coming passion.

I held Erik's head to my breast as he worshiped me with clever lips and tongue. My hips danced underneath him, searching, hungry.

"Fleur." Arne stood over us, eyes shining.

I reached for him. "Arne, please. I need. I need—" I gasped as Erik caught my nipple between his teeth. Heat pooled at the apex of my legs. If the warriors didn't give me relief soon, I would cry.

Erik stopped biting me. His tongue laved the hurt. He rolled to his back with me still in his arms. I sat up and straddled him, tearing his loincloth away.

Arne's hands cradled my hips. "Very well, little she wolf. We will give you what we need."

Erik cupped my breasts, reverence in his expression. Slowly I sank down on him. My pussy spasmed as he filled me. I collapsed forward on him, trembling at the sensations rocking my body. He felt so good, so right. I would never, never tire of the feeling. I was made for him.

My warriors muttered these things to me. Arne stayed crouched behind me, steadying my body as I straightened and started to ride Erik's cock. My body undulated in a movement as old as time.

Arne's hand pushed me forward. His thick fingers

stretched my ass. "You will take me, too, Fleur." His fingers and Erik's cock rubbed my most intimate parts until I shivered at the sensation.

"We will both claim you. You were made for this."

Pressing myself to Erik's bare chest, I waited for Arne to enter me. Erik lifted my chin and caught my mouth in a savage kiss, full of the days, the months, the years of longing.

"So good. So right. You were made for us."

The broad head of Arne's cock fitted to my bottom hole. He pushed in slowly. I was slick with oil and my own juices, but still moaned as my warriors stretched me to the limit. My nipples pebbled against Erik's firm chest.

Fist in my hair, Arne turned my head so he could capture my mouth. "Mine," he growled, and let me go as he began to rock into me.

Both my warriors moved with me between them.

My tears fell then. My fingers pressed into Erik's strong arms.

"Dinnae cry, lass. We are meant to be together."

I laid my cheek on his chest and let the sobs roll out of me, moved faster and my sniffles became moans, vibrating from deep inside me, overwhelming surges of pleasure each more powerful than the last.

"This is it. This is us," Arne said. His lips found my neck and tongue licked my flesh, once, twice. Teeth bit down.

I climaxed hard, body cramping violently as pleasure sizzled through my mind. My men kept moving.

"Take us, take your mates," Arne commanded.

Erik reared up and sank his teeth in my right shoulder. I shouted as if lightning had struck me. My climax tingling my breasts and cunny. The tattooed warrior shouted as his own hips spasmed, shooting his seed deep inside me. I held on as tight as I could, wishing I could meld our bodies completely.

At my back, Arne pounded faster. My body stretched around him as he took his pleasure. With several harsh grunts, he, too, spent himself.

I petted both men, grabbing at them when they meant to slide out of me, small protests leaving my lips. I wanted them to live inside me.

Arne rolled off me, onto his back. "This is how it is meant to be, always, Fleur."

Erik held me close and licked at the blood on my shoulders. Even now the skin was healing, proof that our bond linked us. Berserker strength poured through my limbs.

I laughed. I would die, feeling the strongest I'd ever felt.

"You will not die," Arne vowed. "We will protect you until our last breath." The big man lifted me and set a cool cloth between my legs. He cleaned me carefully.

Erik lay back and wiped at a little blood leaking from his nose. Just a drop, and he swiped at it quickly, but not before I saw.

"You are dying too," I said. "You've been too long cut off from the pack."

Gunnr let out a whine and laid his head on his paws.

It is your presence that keeps us whole, keeps us sane," Arne said. "If you die, we will follow you. But until then, we will guard you with every ounce of strength we have in us."

I WOKE when the fire was almost out. Rising, I replenished the wood, smiling to myself when a trickle of seed ran down my leg. Even when I dropped a cup of water, my two warriors slept through it as if dead.

I touched the tender skin at my shoulders before dressing and pulling on the fur cloak and picking up the staff. Gunnr was out hunting. I would go to them, and find the Alphas and show them my mating bites. They'd know I accepted my Berserker's claim.

Outside the mist had returned. I clutched the staff and a buzzing sensation ran through my arm. Yseult's gift would lead me to the pack and keep me safe.

After a few minutes of walking, the prickling sensation grew stronger. Shapes loomed ahead in the mist.

I smelled the rotten stench just as I realized the staff was giving me a warning.

Cold, dead hands clamped on my bare arms. Not Berserkers.

The Grey Men.

9

The abbey stood on the curve of a lazy village road, golden fields. A peaceful place, but the closer I got, the more my skin crawled, though, that could be the Grey Men's horrible touch.

My captors hadn't worked to subdue me, but they hadn't needed to. One had pointed at my skull and given me a throbbing headache, and I'd dare not try anything else, lest they try to knock me unconscious. If I stayed alert, perhaps I could escape or fight.

I hung onto the staff. They hadn't wanted to touch it, but Yseult's gift had done nothing to protect me.

And so, resigned to my fate, I didn't struggle. I'd never seen so many of my enemy in one place. Fitting, as they were leading me to my final resting place.

The contingent of Grey Men guided me down the road towards the stone building. We arrived at a great wooden and iron-bound door just as dusk fell. Head pounding, eyes half-closed against the pain, I hung limp in the Grey Man's arms.

The door opened and a burly man in friar's clothes came

onto the stoop. He looked me up and down. "What am I supposed to do with this one? " he snapped. "She looks half dead."

The Grey Men were mostly silent but when they spoke it was in a voice like a stylus scratching slate rock.

"Keep her chained," one said in a sibilant whisper.

"Oh all right," the man motioned them to push me forward. "But you best return quickly. I'm not going to feed her."

His hand locked around my arm, he dragged me through the cool halls to a set of stairs. Once we climbed them, he took a great ring of keys that hung on his belt and unlocked a tower door. Inside the flagstones were lined with hay and there was a chamberpot in the corner. He secured me with a chain to the wall and left.

I pushed to the window, and looked down on the gardens below.

"Help," I tried to call, but my voice was weak.

I tried to use the bond between me and the warriors, but there was nothing. Whatever power the Grey Men had to make me weak, it severed the bond as well. I sank down on the hay.

I woke to a scraping sound—the door opening. Before I could force myself to my feet, clutching the staff as a meager weapon, a young woman with long chestnut hair poked her head in.

"Oh," she said. "I didn't realize anyone was in here. I should've checked." She started to close the door.

"Wait," I cried. "don't go!"

She opened the door, with a furtive glance down the hall, and closed it. "I can stay, but only for a moment. You must be new. I haven't met you yet. I'm Hazel, one of the wards here." She gave a little curtsy.

Wards? Before I could ask what she meant, she motioned to my chained foot.

"Is the sickness upon you?"

"What?"

She flushed. "Do you have an ache inside you? Sometimes it manifests as warmth here," she indicated her breasts, blushing further, "or here." Her hand hovered just under waist level. If she were naked it would hide her mons.

"You mean the heat?" I whispered, and used the staff to push up to my feet. "Listen, Hazel. I am here against my will. The Grey Men—some men grabbed me and brought me here." I shook my ankle and rattled the chain. "You have to help me get free."

Her face twisted as if she wanted to help, but dared not.

I realized the wild sight I must make—bits of straw in my hair, long fur cloak, thick boots and carven staff. A cross between a mad woman and a barbarian queen.

"I'm Fleur of Alba," I offered.

"Well met, Fleur of Alba," Hazel said softly. She had very fine manners, and an intelligence behind her sweet mien. "Did your family send you? The friar collects girls who are filled with wanton spirits. He uses this room to calm them when the fever is upon them. They stay here until suitable husbands can be found."

I stilled. "Is that why you're here?"

"No, I am an orphan. There are many of us the friar has taken in. Children of wanton women. We are kept until the time comes when we suffer from the fever, and then the friar finds husbands for us as well."

"Have you ever suffered from the fever?"

Again, the chestnut head darted to glance in the hall behind her. "Yes," Hazel whispered. "I do not know why I trust you, but I do. I have suffered each moon since last summer. But I and a few of the others hide it. One of the girls was sent to a husband, and wound up dead. I overheard the friar talking to the guards about it. Now none of us wish to marry."

"Hazel, you must listen to me. I, too, come from a family of women who go into heat. I was meant to marry, but was taken by the Grey Men, who brought me here. They are evil, and I believe I am in danger." I gulped, hoping I did not sound like a crazy woman. I'd never been encouraged to speak of magic and evil, not until I met my mates. If this young, sheltered woman did not believe me, I would have no hope.

"You called them Grey Men...you mean the pale guards? The strange, silent ones that work for the friar?" Fear reflected on her face. She, too, was affected by the Grey Men, though she might not see them as I did, in their true form.

"Yes. Please, will you help me get free?"

She hesitated, one hand still on the door.

"I know this sounds like madness, but—"

"No," she said, finally coming forward. "It is not madness. I have long suspected the friar is up to no good. I will help you if I can."

"Thank you. Once I get free, I will do all I can to help you."

"First things first. I must find a way to get you free."

As she knelt and examined my shackle, I sent a silent prayer to the goddess for sending a practical, if gentle-natured, aide.

"Hazel," I asked, "The young women who live here—do they all suffer from these fevers?"

"Yes," she frowned. "Some less frequently than others, but mine come on for a few days around the full moon. I've been able to hide my sickness so the friar will not lock me in this room." A door creaked, and she jumped, rushing back to the hall. "I must go, but I will return as soon as I can. Be well, Fleur."

The door clicked shut. I sagged onto the hay.

Hazel, the girls playing in the garden, and the rest of the young women she mentioned: they were all spaewives. The Grey Men were gathering them here. One by one, their heat came upon them, and they were locked away until the Grey Men came to take them to the Corpse King as brides.

And I was next.

THE NEXT TIME the door open, the bulky man in friar's robes came in, dragging Hazel. "You think I wouldn't know you came in here, snooping around?"

He threw her onto the hay and she let out a frightened cry.

"And you," he pointed at me. "The king's men are coming for you. I won't be having you stir up trouble any longer."

I rose to my feet, staff in hand, and advanced as far as the chain would allow. Hazel scuttled behind me.

The friar pointed a fat finger at me. "They're taking you both now, and you won't survive." The door shook as he slammed it behind him.

"I'm sorry, Fleur," Hazel said. Her arms had bruises where the thug had dragged her, and she was trembling. "I did my best. I told a few of the girls you were being held here, and that something was wrong. One of them must have told the friar I put herbs in his drink to make a sleeping draught. Now they're all locked in the dormitory, and we're both captive here."

"It's all right," I said. "There's still time to escape."

But as the sun slanted through our only window, my hopes sank with it.

Hazel told me of her life at the abbey. Most of her time she spent growing things, or weaving clothes to wear or sell at the market. The young women excelled at crafts, and all of them knew how to make herbs thrive. She told me the names of her closest friends.

"Most of us came to the orphanage as babes, and were named for plants. I'm Hazel, and I'm the same age as Sage, Angelica, and Fern. We older ones take care of the younger girls."

"They sound lovely." I kept my eyes half-closed against the light, to protect my throbbing head. The pain seemed to increase with time, as if my body sensed the Grey Men coming near.

"Our life is simple, but it is good. I thought the friar kept us safe, but I've long questioned whether he has our best intentions at heart."

A troubled look crossed her sweet face as she explained. "There was a girl named Sari, who started having fevers and making moon eyes at all the village men. She told me she wanted to run away with one of them. The night she'd planned to go, she disappeared. I thought she'd gone as she'd sworn she would, but when I saw the man in the market, he was dejected and alone. He asked me about her, and that was when I knew something was wrong."

"Do you think the Grey Men came and took her?" My voice had grown hoarse after many hours without food or drink.

"I don't know. I've seen them around, but never inside

the abbey. I thought the friar had hired them to protect us." She rose and paced the room. "I trusted too long. I listened when we were taught that our true nature was evil and must be suppressed." Her hands curled into fists. "If I had paid attention to my instincts, I could've found the truth sooner. I could've saved Sari. I failed my sisters."

I heard a heavy step on the stairs outside our cell door, and pushed to my feet.

"Hazel, if anything happens to me when we are taken to this...evil king...promise me you will do all you can to survive."

She came to clutch my hand. Was I supporting her or was she supporting me? "Surely this cannot mean our death."

"I do not know what it means for you," I said, "but whatever magic this evil king has, it makes me sick. The mere presence of his servants weakens me."

"I will help you." She hugged me.

"No," I said. "If you can get free, take the staff and run. It will guide you to someone who can help." I prayed the witch's tool would either draw Yseult or the Berserkers. "Before the Grey Men took me, I was with a group of men, warriors who are powerful enough to stand against almost anything on this island. Three of them cared for me enough to pledge their life to me. They will want to help you and your friends."

"And you. They will come for you," Hazel reassured me, but I no longer had the strength to answer as the door swung open.

10

The first thing our captor did was slap the staff out of my hands and snap it in half over his knee. It broke like an ordinary stick, and the last of my hope swirled away.

He slapped Hazel when she screamed and tried to fight.

"The money I'm paid isn't enough to deal with this. Next troublemaker, I'll throw out of the tower," he grumbled as he approached us with rags and rope. Using his great strength and girth, he made short work of binding our hands and feet, and gagged us. He covered our heads with sacks and carried us down from the tower to hand us over to the Grey Men. I sagged and lost consciousness when the evil creatures laid their hands on me. Their magic or their evil stench rolled over me, dragging me under.

When I woke, Hazel and I lay together on rough boards that bounced over a road. We were being transported in a wagon. The gag had loosened and I rubbed my mouth on my shoulder to get it to fall, but once it was gone I had nothing to say. Hazel tucked close to me, her hands finding mine behind my back. I was weakened, but awake enough to know when her fingers began to try to untie my bonds.

The wagon bounced horribly on a rock; I struck my head on the boards and everything went dark.

FINGERS FUMBLED AT MY NECKLINE, and I winced away, trying to fight as I regained consciousness. My body was upright, tied so I could not move anything but my head.

A Grey Man was trying to undo the torc around my neck, and hissed when his hands touched the silver. I almost gagged from his fetid breath on my face. The decayed stench was closer. I wondered if the Grey Men were even alive, or men long dead whose bodies had been animated by the Corpse King's dreadful magic.

The thing kept trying to grip my torc, and drawing back as if the silver burned his skin. I would remember that.

It took three Grey Men to try in succession, but they removed the torc and threw it down. I almost cried out at the loss. My body was weakened not only from the attack of the Grey Men, but the lack of connection with my strong warriors. They had been the buffer, keeping me well and strong enough to bear my visions. Why had I fought the bond for so long? Why had I feared my own power, and theirs? If I had embraced their loving dominance over me, I would still be thriving in their care.

Arne, Erik, I tried to link. *Help me.* It was probably too late to call for help, but I would die knowing I did all I could to remain their mates.

The Grey Men had brought Hazel and me to a damp, dimly lit place. When I tried to twist my body, bonds held me fast. The ropes tied me to a post in a cave, halfway between the cobwebbed entrance and a great pile of rocks leading up to a stone slab I'd seen in my visions. On the cairn lay a body wrapped in burial cloth, the fabric grey with age.

The place smelled like it hadn't been opened in a thousand years.

The Grey Men moved through the shadows, ignoring their captives.

Magic moved in this place, thick and cloying, choking me like a thousand locusts covering me.

With my pained head and skin crawling with magic, I welcomed death. It would be a mercy.

I almost smiled, thinking of how Arne and Erik would shout at me for giving up. Even now I heard echoes of their voices in my head, calling my name, telling me to fight.

I focused, and heard Hazel crying. The Grey Men had tied her to the same post by a rope around her neck. Her feet were still hobbled and hands bound behind her, but that wasn't the source of her distress.

"What's wrong?" I rasped.

"Sari. She's here."

The missing girl's crumpled form lay at the foot of the stone pyre. One of the Grey Men took the body's arm and dragged it away. Hazel sobbed louder. The dead body looked ancient and shrunken, cheeks hollow and face as grey as the figure dragging it. Sari had been drained of all blood, and now the Grey Man took the body away to make room for ours.

"What is this place?" Hazel quavered, sounding like she was trying to hold back her sobs. I was grateful my fellow captive had some wits about her, and was struggling to be brave. "What is to become of us?"

Arne had told me of the place where the evil king rests.

The Grey Men must've brought us here in the wagon. I licked my lips, trying to draw some saliva into my mouth so I could answer.

"They are going to revive him." They would use my blood and Hazel's. Eventually the Corpse King would have enough blood, he'd come alive, and he had an abbey full of women waiting for him to breed or sacrifice for more power. Everything the witch feared would come true.

Yseult, I called. *Whatever magic you have to help me, I need it now.*

The next moment, the piece of staff was in my hand.

"Hazel," I croaked, and tried to saw at the rope binding me. I stabbed myself with the splintered staff a few times before she ventured closer.

"Here." She took it somehow and found a way to cut through her ropes. The Grey Men were no longer moving through the tomb, though a few waited beside the pyre, staring up the mummified figure with their unblinking eyes. They did not pay attention to us even when Hazel let out a small gasp in triumph as the last of her bonds broke.

She pressed her body close to the post, hiding her free hands as she worked to undo my bindings.

"No," I protested. I was too weak to run. "Go. I'll distract them. Take the staff and run."

"Fleur—" She bit her lip, tears filling her eyes. "I'll bring back help."

"Go," I whispered to her, and once she had slunk away to the shadows on the side of the cave, I started muttering under my breath.

"Erik, Arne, Gunnr..." I repeated their names over and over, my voice slowly growing louder. My head throbbed with intense pain. Two of the Grey Men standing in front of the stone pile turned to look at me. This time, their gimlet eyes didn't affect me at all.

"Erik, Arne, Gunnr," I chanted like a witch at a rite. Outside rose a hissing sound; the Grey Men were angry. I closed my eyes, hoping Hazel had gotten away. My lips kept mouthing my mate's names.

"Stop."

I opened my eyes and a Grey Man was pointing at me as if to cast a spell. Still whispering my mates names, I waited for the pain, and...nothing.

"Erik, Arne, Gunnr," I cried louder. The Grey Man hissed, and more of the hideous creatures came to untie me. They dragged me towards the cairn.

I screamed my mate's names with the last of my strength.

Fleur? Relief rushed through me at Arne's voice.

I'm here. For the first time since the Grey Men took me, my head was clear.

We are coming for you. We are close enough to hear and link with you—it won't be long before we are at your side. Energy surged through me as my men poured their power into the bond. They would uphold me until the last.

Tears pricked my eyes as I responded, *No, stay away. It isn't safe.*

The Grey men brought me closer to the figure wrapped on the stone slab. My skin crawled as I realized it was moving. The Corpse King was coming to life.

My feet dragged and I began to fight.

How many times must we tell ye—we'd risk any danger to be at your side?

I am dying, I told them. *It is the end. Do not waste your life. I can die alone.*

Little flower, a new voice growled in my head. The sound was barely human, but clear nonetheless. *Since we met you, you haven't been alone. You will never be alone.*

The Grey Men pushed me close to the ancient king. Next to the body was a helmet and breastplate, and a sword.

I struggled and got one arm free, reaching for the weapon.

Hang on, Fleur. Arne said. *You're strong. You've been a target of this evil all your life.*

Under my bare arm, the corpse licked its lips. I jerked back, and a Grey Man grabbed my shoulder, wrenching me back. It held a wicked knife it wanted to set at my throat.

Fight! Erik's cry turned into a roar.

Berserker rage powered my limbs. Half leaning on the stone slab, I twisted and kicked at the knife-wielding creature. The force of my blow broke my attacker in half. Its dry and rotten body broke into pieces that the other Grey Men dragged away. More hands reached for me , but I snarled and kept kicking to fend them off.

Under me, the Corpse King moved. An arm clamped around me.

I screamed. The dead thing was too strong. It pulled me face to face, and its servants' hands grabbed and held me. I fought like a wild thing, but in my struggles, my hand scraped on the chain mail.

With the speed of a striking snake, the creature in grave clothes grabbed my wrist and brought it to its lips.

Pain howled through me as it drank, and my mind opened to the awful link.

Hello, my bride.

Nauseous and bleeding, I couldn't fight. The creature kept sucking on my wrist, and its evil bond took hold.

Get out of her head, my warriors roared. *She's ours.*

The thing recoiled.

Blood is spoiled, it hissed.

"Arne," I shrieked, "Erik, Gunnr!"

I reached out and suddenly held the second piece of Yseult's staff.

My arm reared back and snapped forward to drive the sharpened stake into its chest.

The thing caught my wrist, its grip monstrously strong.

We're coming, Fleur!

I ripped my arm away. The Corpse King was too strong to fight. Still clutching the staff, I ran.

Grey Men reached out, trying to catch me, but the Corpse King bellowed, and all his servants staggered.

I made it to the edge of the cave, just in time to greet a giant, golden eagle dropping from the sky.

Fleur!

Arne. I staggered, and Grey Men started closing in on me. There were hundreds of them milling about in front of the cave.

Run! I'll clear a path, Arne swooped and dove, eagle's claws clutching the creatures blocking my path. Two swoops of its wings and it gained enough height to drop the struggling Grey Man onto its compatriots, using one body to take out three more.

I ran, dodging around boulders, trying to avoid Grey Men as I made for the treeline, but it seemed so far away. Nothing grew in a wide area around this evil place.

In front of the cave, the Grey Men swarmed around a large pile of swords and weapons. They lifted them, ready for battle. A thicket of spears raised to the skies, keeping Arne at bay. I looked for a way out, but there were too many of them, and the ranks were closing.

A group of them cornered me against a large rock.

"Stay back," I shouted, in a voice too hoarse to be heard. I swayed on my feet.

A wolf burst through the line of Grey Men. Snarls brought chills to my arms.

Gunnr fought to my side. His great teeth ripped at the creatures.

They taste disgusting, and smell worse. The wolf paused to give me a mournful look.

They are the Corpse King's servants, and not much more than corpses themselves, Arne said.

Erik broke through to me, leaving a trail of disembodied parts of Grey Men in his wake. He had an axe, and wore only a loincloth. Shouting his battle cry, he sent his weapon crashing into the animated dead men, and howled his rage.

Gunnr fought with tooth and claw. He snapped at the Grey Men, and reared up on hind legs to drive them off, but there was always another to take its place. More streamed out of the woods to the mouth of the cave, backing us up against the boulder.

There are too many. I clutched my piece of staff, and wished I had more of a weapon.

We will stand with ye, Fleur. Just promise that you willnae leave us again.

Never, I vowed. I stood surrounded by the enemy, body weak and hair matted with dust and cobwebs, fur cloak and boots dirty and torn, holding a splintered carven staff. But I was with my loves, and I was happier than I'd ever been.

We stand together.

We may not survive, but we will kill as many as we can, and we die trying to kill that thing.

It drank my blood. I tried to fight, but I woke it.

No wonder the Grey Men wanted you. You're powerful

enough to kill the Corpse King, if you're powerful enough to bring it to life.

We will stand with ye. It'll be a grand tale for the bards.

The circle of Grey Men tightened around us, and the men readied themselves for their last stand.

An eerie sound sent shivers up my arms.

What is that?

It grew closer, a great howling noise, louder and stronger than a storm wind.

Wolves?

Erik shook his head, a fierce grin on his face. "Berserkers."

He pulled me close.

The pack has come, Arne said.

The first shock waves hit, Grey Men tossed in the air. Body parts rained down on their compatriots.

A Grey Man darted closer to me and Gunnr snapped at him.

Hold on, Arne said. *They are turning the tide. The Alphas lead the charge.*

The Grey Men surrounding us turned to face the oncoming enemy. They were trapped, pinned between two savage forces. With a subtle hissing sound, they were torn apart.

But more evil servants ran to take their place. Erik drew me up onto a rock and I saw the pack—rank upon rank of Berserkers, all in monstrous form. They tore through the ranks of Grey Men like a spear cleaves water. Whatever magic possessed the Corpse King's servants, it made them impervious to fear, but the Grey Men couldn't stand against the bellowing warriors, who attacked with the ferocity of starving wolves.

"Yseult spoke the truth. Berserkers were made to fight this evil," Erik said.

I tugged on his arm. "The pack. They want to kill you."

"Yes," he said. "They'll save us first. Run!"

Grey Men marched to line up in front of the cave, ready to defend the Corpse King. They ignored us as we raced for the trees.

A Berserker reared up in front of us, and Erik pushed me behind him. The tattooed warrior charged, tackling the slavering monster. With savage strength, he sent the opposing Berserker into a knot of Grey Men. The Berserker started fighting them instead.

"Fleur, go," Erik pointed to the woods with blood tipped claws. I obeyed, limping with exhaustion until the black wolf pushed in front of me.

Climb on, Gunnr ordered.

Clutching his fur, I did and rode him to the forest.

Behind us, more Berserkers tried to attack Erik. Arne swooped and distracted them while he ran.

They need to fight the Grey Men, not us, I thought in frustration. My mouth was too dry to speak.

Their beast knows nothing but the battle, Gunnr told me. *And more than victory over the evil they don't understand, they want to possess you.*

I gripped his fur tighter as he darted into the wood.

A great crash rang out behind us, my ears filled with the sound of rocks falling.

The cave has collapsed, Arne reported.

Dust rolled over the fighting creatures.

Maybe the Corpse King will be crushed.

The warriors didn't say anything, but their answer was in the grim silence that followed. Not even Yseult knew what would kill the Corpse King.

The Alphas are calling everyone to follow our trail, Arne warned as Gunnr fled with me on his back.

Erik caught up with us in a thicket.

"I've got her," he lifted me. "I'll take her to the camp."

"She needs care," Arne told him.

"No," I rasped on a dry throat. "We need to escape."

"Hush," Erik said. He ducked under thick pine branches. "We know what ye need."

I studied his face as he ran wildly on a path of his own making. He looked beaten and tired, but his eyes burned gold.

How did you find me?

"You did not call to us at first," he chastened. "We waited and searched the area, when Arne realized the grey men had taken you we knew you might appear at the center of the evil he sensed. We headed here, and would've been here sooner if we hadn't had to evade the pack."

I'm sorry.

"It's over lass. And it will never happen again."

We came to a stream and followed it to a waterfall.

"Here," he said. He brought me right to the bank. Cupping his hands he brought water to my lips. "Drink."

I sucked down all I could, and he repeated the action twice before I could speak.

When he brought water to my lips a third time, I shook my head.

"More," he insisted. "Ye look like death. Ye survived the fight."

I thought I saw my death, but it was the Corpse King.

"Ye did nearly die," he reminded me. "But you're safe again. Drink more for me, and I will get a fire going to make broth. I will bathe ye soon."

"There is no time," I told him. "You must escape."

"We're not leaving you and you're not leaving us, even if I have to tie you again."

Erik carried me to the bedroll after I had drunk my fill.

"Erik—"

He lifted the rope in threat and I sagged back.

"No, I'll behave."

"Good lass." He handed me a skein of mead. "Drink some of that, slowly. Arne and Gunnr are scouting, protecting us. They will try to mislead the pack."

As I sipped, he built a small fire and heated water.

I blinked awake when he dabbed a warm cloth about my face.

"You have not been cared for."

He washed me carefully and smeared oil on my cracked lips.

I told him of my sojourn away from them. "There is a girl, Hazel. The Grey Men brought her from the abbey with me. She ran for help."

"The pack will find her."

"She will be frightened."

"She will learn there is nothing to fear."

At the tenderness in his voice, I leaned into his palm.

"I'm sorry I ran," I told him.

He stroked my hair.

"You're safe now. We will care for you."

Storm clouds gathered overhead. Lightning and thunder rumbling in the distance, coming from the place we'd just left. The trees swayed in the wind.

"There is evil on the wind. The Corpse King lives, and will rally his forces to regain his strength. This place is dangerous to stay. We will get you out of here."

"No, we will."

I startled at the strange voice.

One of the Alphas walked from the trees. Erik rose but stood with hands at his sides.

Erik, run, I cried.

"No, Fleur. Stay calm."

I looked about wildly, but we were surrounded.

11

"Take him," the Alpha growled.

"No." My cries were lost in the answering snarls of the other Berserkers.

Two warriors each grabbed Erik.

"Stop," I grabbed up the piece of Yseult's staff and pushed to my feet.

A Berserker reached for me and I shrank back, ready to stab him.

An eagle screamed and landed close, turning into Arne.

"Don't touch her," he shouted before the Berserkers mobbed him.

"Are you all right, Fleur?" the Alpha asked.

"Listen to me," I said. "These men are my mates. You cannot kill them."

"They took what was not theirs. We will have a hearing, and you will be allowed to speak."

Be calm, Fleur. We have a plan.

Out loud, Erik said, "Ye have our word, Alpha. We will not run. But Fleur needs to be away from this evil place."

After some deliberation, the Alphas made a stretcher for

me and carried me themselves. My mates disappeared, surrounded by the rest of the pack.

Gunnr had slipped away. Arne could get free and become an eagle, but what of Erik?

No more running, Arne said.

"Are you well, Fleur?" One of the Alphas mated to Brenna asked. "Did the rogue warriors hurt you?"

"They cared for me. They loved me. They have done nothing wrong."

He frowned. "You do not look well."

Swaying on the stretcher, I explained to the Alphas all I knew of the Corpse King, the Grey Men and my experience at the tomb.

Enough talking, Arne admonished me. *You need to rest.*

I will not let them kill you.

You have given them much to think about. Let them deliberate while you sleep and become strong.

I closed my eyes, lulled by my mate's voice. The Alphas picked up the pace, running before a strange howling in the trees, an angry voice punishing us for depriving it of its prey.

I WOKE IN THE LODGE, surrounded by my sisters.

"Fleur," Sabine and Muriel cried.

As soon as I drank enough to wet my throat, I asked, "Where's Arne and Erik?" I'd tried to reach them via the bond, and had no answer. As far as I knew, Gunnr had escaped, and was staying away.

Sabine pressed her lips together.

"I need to see them." I pushed up, ignoring my sister's protests. I ran out of the lodge, stopping at the sight of two burly guards.

"Where are my mates?" I demanded, no longer caring whether the pack punished me for insolence.

"The traitors are under guard. They are being punished," one growled.

"Come back, Fleur." Sabine wrapped her arms around me. Swaying on weak limbs, I let her help me back inside.

"I want to see them. Are they injured?"

"Berserkers heal quickly. They are only in a little pain," Muriel said.

"This isn't fair."

"Come, eat and drink. We have water for you to bathe."

As soon as I'd renewed my strength, I dressed in clean clothes along with the fur cloak and the boots. I found an eagle feather tattered on the ground, and put it in my hair. Thus adorned, I refused to eat or drink anymore until I saw my mates.

Muriel's mates escorted me to the Alphas.

The air was still chilled as if midsummer had fled before the power of the Corpse King.

One of the Alphas mated to Brenna sat presiding. A burly blond Viking, he was considered the wisest of the Berserkers.

I marched right up to him. "You must release my mates. You cannot separate us. I will die without them."

"You nearly died with them," a second Alpha muttered.

"Explain, Fleur," the blond beckoned.

"We are bonded. That is how they found me when the Corpse King's servants kidnapped me."

"And how did the Corpse King come to possess you in the first place?"

"I was foolish and left. I will not leave again."

The Alphas exchanged glances.

"You said I can choose." My fists clenched at my side to keep from railing at them all. "I choose them."

"Fleur," the Alpha sighed. "These warriors are unstable. We feared they would take you, and they did."

"I belong to them," I whispered.

"The pack requires proof of the bond."

What can we give as proof? I reached for my mates, but heard nothing. Panic must've crossed my face, because the Alpha leaned forward.

"I am sorry, Fleur--"

"You cannot keep me from them," I cried out. Samuel motioned and another Alpha started to restrain me.

"Stop," a voice rang out. "You will not touch her."

The Alpha frowned but backed away.

Fleur, be calm. I am here. I stilled at the voice, strangely familiar. A black-haired man pushed through the throng of warriors. His hair and beard was long and shaggy, and he wore only a pelt over his shoulders and a loincloth around his waist.

"Who is this?" Samuel straightened.

"I do not recognize him," another Alpha murmured.

"Nor do I," said Muriel's mate.

I started forward eagerly, and the warriors around me parted, though they still blocked the strange wolf's path. "Please," I reached for my mate. "Let him through."

The blond Alpha motioned, and the wolves withdrew their weapons.

Gunnr pushed forward and I reached for him. He lifted me in his arms, and I knew I'd felt their hold before, even if only in my dreams.

"I recognize your face," I whispered. "I dreamt of you."

"And I, you," Gunnr pressed his forehead against mine.

"Do not be dismayed, little flower. All of your mates will return to you."

"Who are you?" the Alpha asked, and Gunnr turned to him,

"I who was once a wolf. I am a man."

"You said I could choose," I repeated. "I choose Gunnr, Arne and Erik."

"The bond is working," Muriel's mate said. "These three warrior brothers are stable."

"The pack will not think it fair," another Alpha muttered.

"The pack will be too busy saving an abbey of spaewives from the Corpse King," Gunnr said.

"What?" several warriors spoke all at once. "There are more spaewives? Alpha, is this true?"

Samuel sighed. "We have sent scouts, but have not told the pack of this possibility, yet."

A burly warrior pushed closer to the blond Alpha's throne. "If there are women for us, we want to know."

"Particularly if they are threatened by this evil," added another.

"Send us to rescue them, Alpha," growled a third. "We are ready."

Samuel held up his hand. "Enough. I am ready to send the pack to save these women from their fate. Rolf, Leif, Brokk," he addressed the three warriors mobbing him, "you will lead the charge." He told the assembled warriors of the Corpse King's past, and the awful source of his power. "He sent his servants far and wide to gather women in readiness for his return. That is why they plagued Fleur and her sisters. They probably would've taken them, if she had not resisted for so long."

"So it is true?" Rolf asked. "There's an entire abbey full of women who could be mates to the Berserkers?"

"It's true," I confirmed. "I was there. My friend Hazel will tell you, once she is found."

"Hazel?" Leif spoke up, and laughed. "That is the name of the little rabbit Knut found running from the cave."

Samuel looked at me. "A young woman with part of the witch's staff—is she your friend?"

"Yes," I said, "is she safe?"

The warriors all looked amused. "She is," Leif said. "Knut may not be for all the trouble she's giving him. She's tried to stab him several times."

"She will calm down if she sees me. I'll tell her not to fight so much," I said.

"The fight is half the fun." One of the Alphas smirked, and nudged his mate Sabine, who swatted at him.

Gunnr gave me a quiet smile.

"If all the women at the abbey are like her, there will be plenty of worthy Berserker brides," Samuel mused. "The entire pack could be mated by winter solstice."

"You must move quickly," Gunnr said. "The Grey Men will come for these women, soon."

Every warrior in the clearing straightened. Several put hands to their weapons.

"Very well," Samuel nodded and signaled to Rolf, Leif and Brokk. "Let us plan the rescue. Bring forth the woman Hazel, and we will consult her as to the best plan of attack."

"Alpha," Gunnr said softly.

"Yes." Samuel smiled and turned to me. "Fleur, your bravery has won you your mates. Gunnr, take her home."

～

Gunnr wasted no time carrying me down the mountain to the lodge.

"Where are Arne and Erik?" I asked.

"Coming. The pack had taken them far away, beyond where the bond allowed you to speak to them."

"Why?"

"They were being punished as payment for our sins."

"What?"

"Don't worry, Fleur. They are all right, and even now are returning to us." He strode faster when the lodge came into sight. "In the meantime, I have something I wish to do." He claimed my mouth even as he kicked the door open. My sisters had left the place decorated with flowers for my return. Scented wood burned in the fire pit.

Gunnr made straight for the bed and lay me down.

"Gunnr," I gasped as his mouth ventured lower. "Shouldn't we wait for the others?"

"No," he said and quickly kissed his way from my jaw to my breasts.

I soon stopped complaining. My body writhed under him, ready.

"Quick, quick." I drew his loincloth away and took his hot length in hand.

"Slowly," he gasped. "I have to be gentle."

"No," I growled, jacking his cock with one hand while the other fumbled with my skirts.

Gunnr took both my wrists and set them firmly on the bed beside my shoulders.

"I have waited for this my whole life," he told me. "We go at my pace."

"Gunnr." My heart twisted.

"Let me look at you." He drew back.

I studied him as he studied me. There was a scar on his face, right where the white patch of fur was on the wolf's muzzle.

He drew apart my legs with maddening slowness. I was so ready for him, honey dripped from my center.

He covered me with his body.

"Please," my legs wrapped around his hips. "I need you."

Sweat beaded on his forehead as he sank slowly into me.

"It's too much. I can't go slowly," he gasped.

"I don't want you to," I said, and as he moved faster and faster, I reared up and bit him.

Tasted blood on my lips.

"Little wolf," he smiled. Wrapping my hair around one of his hands, he tugged my head back. Bending, he sank his fangs into my throat.

White hot pleasure whipped through me. I panted through my climax, only to realize that he had taken his.

"Again?"

He chuckled. "My warrior brothers are waiting outside. They wanted us to be together. Are you ready to take all of us?"

I dug my hands into his hair as I would his fur.

"Yes." I kissed him.

Arne and Erik came to either side, already naked. Whatever wounds they had sustained had already healed. My own body felt charged and ready, the power of my Berserker mates flowing through me.

Gunnr positioned me so I was straddling him. His big hands never left my body, as if reluctant to stop touching me.

Arne knelt on the bed and added his soothing strokes to my back, then pushed me down. Erik squeezed my bum before dripping oil into the crack of my ass. His finger brushed my back crinkle and wormed inside.

"Tight," Erik huffed. "She is not ready."

I growled at him.

"You'll be lucky if we don't make ye wear the plug day and night, until ye remember to obey." He palmed my bottom cheek and squeezed hard in warning. "Ye ran from us. Ye will be punished."

"Not now," Arne said. "When you have regained your strength."

"Perhaps she is not strong enough to bed all of us now," Gunnr said.

"No," I twisted, grabbing both Arne and Erik's arms, while pressing my weight down on Gunnr below me. "Please take me, my loves. My mates."

"Verrae well," Erik said in a teasing tone, coming to kneel on the bed on the other side of me. His cock jutted out from his lean hips, bobbing enticingly. "But only if ye are verrae, verrae good."

"I will be, I promise."

Arne directed me with a hand on my back and a stern order, "Suck him."

I bent and took Erik's rod in my mouth, licking and tasting him as best I could.

"Now him," Erik commanded.

With hands in my hair, the warriors guided me from one cock to another while my hips rocked, sliding my greedy center over Gunnr's firm body.

"Enough," Gunnr said, and rolled so I was under him again. Without warning, he impaled me on his still hard cock.

Arne and Erik knelt closer so they could fondle a breast each as I took their cocks in hand. I jerked their huge members as Gunnr pumped inside me. The lodge filled with the thick scent of our arousal. The cradle of my hips tightened, drawing Gunnr's cock further inside me.

My climax broke over me again when they splashed me with their seed.

12

For two days a strange storm raged over the center of the island. The pack scouts reported that it centered over the place of the Corpse King. The entire pack made ready for another battle, but left the four of us alone. Arne and Erik made no mention of what the pack had done to punish them, but apparently their suffering had been great enough that they didn't link with me for fear of the pain spilling through the bond.

"The pack law must be satisfied. Any wolf who steps out of bounds opens himself to discipline or banishment," Gunnr told me. "We knew that when we took you."

"Will you be punished?" I asked him.

"No," he said. "Being a wolf for as long as I was is punishment enough."

I'd slept every night in his arms. My mates cared for me as they had before, and I thrived.

Hazel came to visit me. She'd been rescued from the Grey Men and claimed by a giant blond warrior named Knut. By the way the big Berserker looked at her and she at him, I knew that they were mated.

"Fleur, I am so glad to see you. They told me that you were rescued. I met your sisters," she spoke all in a rush, and hugged me hard. "I wasn't sure you would survive," she whispered in my ear.

"I did not know either," I told her. "But my mates never gave up searching for me."

"You look much, much better," she said.

"We care for her," Arne rumbled.

Erik tugged my braid. "We will not let her run again."

"Good," Hazel said and dipped her head close to mine again. "I don't know how you manage three mates. I have found it difficult with just one." She drew back and met my eyes uncertainly, and I decided I would kick all my men out of the lodge one night, and invite all my sisters along with Hazel to swap secrets of handling our large mates.

"Difficult but rewarding," Knut hovered over Hazel, caressing her shoulders with his huge, battle scarred hands.

She smiled up at him, and covered his hand with hers, and I knew she'd be all right.

"The Alphas have decided to rescue the women in the abbey," Arne told me once Hazel and her mate had left. "Even now most of the pack makes ready for the spaewives. The Berserkers are eager to claim their mates."

"The women will need time to adjust to pack life. They will be afraid."

"We have no doubt you and your sisters will rush to greet them and allay their fears," Arne said. "But these things take their course."

I hoped the Berserkers would not burst into the abbey and carry off all the women the same way my mates had done me, but had to agree.

Erik tugged my braid again. "You are feeling much better, right, Fleur?"

"Yes." I frowned and shifted on my plugged bottom. Erik had insisted on inserting the wooden bulb that morning. I couldn't ignore the stretched and stuffed feeling. Sitting was bad enough, but walking was worse—I felt like I waddled. Whenever the men looked at me, I blushed.

"We've decided you are well enough for your punishment," Erik grinned at me.

"Oh no." I tried to run, but tattooed arms scooped me right up.

He held me while Arne and Gunnr bound me quickly.

I ended up face down arms stretched above my head. They bound my calves to my thighs as they had when they made me their little pet.

I growled into the furs, and one of them swatted my bottom, then stroked my lower lips. Slap, touch, slap, touch, until I was panting.

"Do ye know why we punish ye this way?" Erik tapped the plug and I yelped. "Because with a sore and plugged arse, ye cannae forget who ye belong to."

I huffed and Erik spanked me one more time, and left so Gunnr could take his place.

"My turn to punish you," Gunnr told me. He played with the plug, pushing and twisting it in my backside until my face burned and my cunny dripped.

"Please," I begged.

"I have not even touched you."

"She's wet from embarrassment," Erik reported.

"Here, Fleur." Arne knelt in front of me, with a silver ring in his hands. "This torc will lock around your neck. It cannot be removed but by our hands." He put it into place.

"Now we can leash ye and lead ye around in front of the entire pack," Erik teased.

"You wouldn't dare," I whined.

Gunnr answered for him, smacking one of my bottom cheeks and then the other. He disciplined me until I was squirming, and massaged the sting away.

"Good lass," he murmured. "Now for your real punishment."

A snapping sound, and a sharper pain pricked my backside, like the quick sting of a wasp. I yelped and plunged forward into the pelts.

"Oh no," Arne flipped me over and held my upper half. Erik tied my legs open.

I tested the bonds, my legs straining as Gunnr approached holding the long stick tipped with a flap of leather.

He snapped it against my right inner thigh and frowned. "It leaves a mark." The leather flap left a small red patch on my sensitive inner thigh. "I do not like it."

"I do," Erik said. "I like seeing our marks on her. That and the plug, makes her feel owned, doesn't it, Fleur?"

Snatching the implement, the tattooed warrior swatted my other thigh.

I twitched.

"I told you, I do not like leaving marks." Gunnr grabbed it from him.

"It'll fade," Arne said.

"Please no more," I said.

"Ye were very naughty, Fleur," Erik wagged a finger at me. "Ye deserve this."

"We must punish her," Arne said to Gunnr. "The beast requires it."

Gunnr toyed with the small piece of leather at the end of the cane.

"You have a choice, Fleur. I will use this to mark you until you understand your place, or we can keep you tied like this," he used the crop to indicate my bound legs, "and play with you as our pet. You will receive no pleasure."

My cunny was throbbing despite—or because of—the pain. "Punish me with that, please," I said. "I can take it."

"Good lass," Erik rubbed his hands together. "Allow me."

Gunnr handed the crop over reluctantly. Erik placed it over my weeping slit.

I sucked in a breath. *Please be gentle.*

"He will," Arne rumbled under me. "We will never truly hurt you."

The leather hovered at my center.

"Breathe, Fleur," Erik admonished me, and waited until I did. Then he used the leather end to rub my folds.

I sighed.

"See? We can give ye pain or pleasure. Or both." He tapped the crop on my pussy, the touches growing with force and intensity.

"Do ye see?" Erik demanded of Gunnr.

"Yes, I do now." Gunnr took the implement back. "Deep breaths, Fleur." He snapped the crop faster on my lower lips, turning them red and puffy. Heat pooled at my center, making me desperate for more stimulation—even the bite of the crop. I whimpered, moaned, and rocked my hips as much as I could.

"You will not disobey us again," Arne said, rolling a nipple between his fingers.

"No, no," I agreed.

Gunnr slapped the crop onto my swollen pussy lips. My whole body jerked and aching pleasure spiraled through me. I cried out.

"Was that a good cry or a bad one?" Gunnr asked.

"Good, it was very good," Erik said, squatting close to me. "See how her cunny creams?" His finger delved into my slick hole before he brought the digit to his mouth and licked it clean.

"I do not want to hurt her." Gunnr hesitated.

"This is a good pain," Arne said. "It teaches her that her body belongs to us. She is ours and completely in our care."

Erik stroked my tender folds. "Such heat," he said as I mewled, my upper half squirming against Arne's massive chest. "Her body begs for the pain."

"Hold her open," Gunnr suggested. "I wish to try something."

"No," I tried to move my legs together, but the ropes held fast.

"Be still," Arne rumbled in my ear. "Be a good girl."

Erik used two fingers to spread my lower lips apart.

"Just the right touch," Gunnr mused. "Not too harsh, but not too gentle either."

He tapped the crop right on my sensitive nub.

I threw back my head and gasped. Painful pleasure rocked my entire body. Sparks went off behind my eyes.

"Again, I think," Gunnr said, and Erik agreed.

He tapped the crop twice, lightly, before slamming it down on my exposed pleasure nub. I cried out as the sharp sting cascaded into ecstasy.

"Now," Arne said. He lifted and turned me. I cried out again as he thrust up inside my hungry body. The two other warriors steadied me, but I clawed at Arne's muscled shoulders. "More, I need you—"

"Patience, little flower."

Gunnr came to my head, stroking back my hair and teasing my lips with his thumb while Erik took out the plug.

Strong hands braced me as Erik eased into my bottom. My insides rippled, waves of pleasure crashing through my overstimulated body.

Gunnr grasped my chin and fed me his cock. I sucked as if my life depended on it, desperate to share the overwhelming sensation.

We feel it. We are with you, Gunnr reminded me. *We are one.*

Erik and Arne began moving, pushing and pulling. Lights burst behind my eyes, shooting stars as I climaxed again and again. There was no barrier between us. I opened my mind and let my intense feelings flow to my men, pushing them to the breaking point.

I chanted their names as they sped their thrusts. Erik, Arne, Gunnr...

Mine, Erik snarled into the bond.

Mine, Gunnr echoed.

"Ours," Arne rumbled.

Ecstasy sizzled through my mind, freezing out any thought. It spilled from me into the bond, making the warriors howl and pump their pleasure into my willing body. I took every bit of their seed, because I was their mate, and I was strong—strong enough to bond to three men, to save them, and to make them whole.

And we were one.

EPILOGUE

The abbey sat on the edge of a lazy curve in the road to the village. A young woman walked the path, the setting sun burnishing her hair. Something moved in the shadows of the woods, and with a fearful look, she scuttled up to the great iron bound door, and disappeared inside.

Deeper inside the woods, rank upon rank of warriors stood waiting and watching.

"This the place where the women are kept?" one asked the scout.

"It is," the scout answered. "And tonight, we take them."

Want more Berserkers? The whole pack needs their mates, and they found an abbey full of spaewives! Read Rescued by the Berserker for Hazel & Knut's story. :)

FREE BOOK

Get two secret Berserker books, Bred by the Berserkers and
A Berserker Birth, available exclusively to you:

A NOTE FROM LEE SAVINO

Hey there. It's me, Lee Savino. I'm so glad you read this book and ordered it directly from my store. Readers like you make my author life possible! And being an author is a dream come true.

If you're like me, you're wondering what to read next. Let me help you out...

If you haven't yet, check out the two exclusive extras I wrote in the Berserker world. They're available here:

Bred by the Berserkers
https://geni.us/BredBerserkerNONL

A Berserker Birth
https://geni.us/BirthBerserkerNONL

And if you want more Berserkers, you can find the complete selection at my store or get the 15 book bundle here!

WANT MORE BERSERKERS?

These fierce warriors will stop at nothing to claim their mates...

Get a 15 e-book Berserker bundle on sale at my Lee Savino shop!

The Berserker Saga

Sold to the Berserkers – Brenna, Samuel & Daegan
Mated to the Berserkers – Brenna, Samuel & Daegan
Bred by the Berserkers (FREE novella only available to you)
– Brenna, Samuel & Daegan
Taken by the Berserkers – Sabine, Ragnvald & Maddox
Given to the Berserkers – Muriel and her mates
Claimed by the Berserkers – Fleur and her mates
Rescued by the Berserker – Hazel & Knut
Captured by the Berserkers – Willow, Leif & Brokk
Kidnapped by the Berserkers – Sage, Thorbjorn & Rolf
Bonded to the Berserkers – Laurel, Haakon & Ulf

ALSO BY LEE SAVINO

For film and TV rights inquiries: **lee.savino@leesavino.com**

Paranormal romance

Berserker Saga

Sold to the Berserkers

Mated to the Berserkers

Bred by the Berserkers (FREE novella only available at www.leesavino.com)

Taken by the Berserkers

Given to the Berserkers

Claimed by the Berserkers

Rescued by the Berserker

Captured by the Berserkers

Kidnapped by the Berserkers

Bonded to the Berserkers

Berserker Babies

Night of the Berserkers

Owned by the Berserkers

Tamed by the Berserkers

Mastered by the Berserkers

Surrendered to the Berserkers

Midnight Doms with Renee Rose

Alpha's Blood

His Captive Mortal

The Virgin and the Vampire

(All Souls' Night anthology exclusive)

Werewolves of Wallstreet with Renee Rose

Big Bad Boss: Midnight

Big Bad Boss: Moon Mad

Sci fi romance

Planet of Kings with Tabitha Black

Brutal Mate

Brutal Claim

Brutal Capture

Brutal Beast

Brutal Demon

Tsenturion Warriors with Golden Angel

Alien Captive

Alien Tribute

Alien Abduction

Dragons in Exile with Lili Zander

Draekon Mate

Draekon Fire

Draekon Heart

Draekon Abduction

Draekon Destiny

Daughter of Draekons

Draekon Fever

Draekon Rogue

Draekon Holiday

Draekon Rebel Force with Lili Zander

Draekon Warrior

Draekon Conqueror

Draekon Pirate

Draekon Warlord

Draekon Guardian

Contemporary Romance

Royally Bad

Royally Fake Fiancé

Her Marine Daddy

Her Dueling Daddies

Beauty & The Lumberjacks

Snowed in with the Lumberjack

Rescuing Regina

Dark Mafia Romance

Mafia Brides

Revenge is Sweet

Vengeance is Mine

A Dark Mafia Romance trilogy with Stasia Black

Innocence

Awakening

Queen of the Underworld

Beauty and the Rose trilogy with Stasia Black

Beauty's Beast

Beauty & the Thorns

Beauty & the Rose

Cowboy Romance

Rocky Mountain Mail Order Brides

Rocky Mountain Dawn

Rocky Mountain Bride

Rocky Mountain Rose

Rocky Mountain Romp

Rocky Mountain Rogue

Rocky Mountain Daddy

Rocky Mountain Ride

Possessing Pearl

Wild Whip Ranch with Tristan River

Cowboy's Babygirl

Taming His Wild Girl

ABOUT THE AUTHOR

USA today bestselling author Lee Savino has written over 69 steamy romance novels. Bad boys, mafia men, wolf shifters, and dragon shifters in space—her dominant, alpha-hole heroes will stop at nothing to possess their one true love. Happily-ever-after and book hangover guaranteed!

Connect with Lee Savino in her fabulous Goddess Group: https://www.facebook.com/groups/LeeSavino